WIZARD FROM THE VALLEY

BOOK ONE

WIZARD OF PROPHECY

BY JAMES BAKER

THIS BOOK IS DEDICATED TO MY
FAMILY AND FRIEND'S
THANK YOU FOR ALL THE SUPPORT

Chapter 1
Escape from the valley

Dolan sat outside the little cottage that was nestled in the valley amid the great mountain range. He sat looking at the stars thinking how very few people even knew that the valley existed at all. But for Dolan, it was all that there was. He knew that there was an entire world out there and at a time he wanted to explore it. He had only been to the little village on the other side of the pass a few times and never for very long. He had gone there with his father to sell goods that they had produced on their small farm.

His mother would make clothes and blankets from wool from their sheep or the skins from animals they trapped or butchered. His parents had taught him to make use of all that he took from the land and to only take what he needed to use.

This would be the first year that he would be taking care of all the planting and harvesting on his own. It had been a harsh winter and his father had taken ill and died. He felt that his mother would have followed his father, if she didn't feel obligated to care for her son. He could see an emptiness in her eyes that seemed to go deep into her soul.

Dolan was seventeen now and felt he could take care of himself. But she had told him that he still had a lot more to learn. He didn't want to lose her by no means. He just hated seeing her so lost. He tried all that he could to fill the void that was left. But he knew he couldn't do that.

Dolan sat lost in thought when he heard the rumbling of a storm moving in as thunder echoed off the mountains surrounding him. He looked to the west and saw the clouds starting to cover the stars. Spring storms could be very destructive in the valley. Often the rain would melt the snow still left on the sides of the mountains, and this combined with the rain would bring on major flooding. They had lost livestock in the past from flash floods. Dolan was glad that all the livestock was safe in the barn that he and his father built. They had spent a whole summer hauling rock and dirt and piling it to build a foundation high enough to keep the floods out of the barn.

Dolan heard a sound behind him and turned to see his mother stepping out of the door to the cottage. She was a tall, beautiful woman in her early forties. Her long dark hair had a few streaks of gray that looked silver in the lamplight. She always had a tender smile on her face, even when she was correcting him for doing wrong. He felt that the thought of disappointing her was worse than having a strap taken to him, which was his father's choice to correct him.

"Are you going to stay out here all night?" she asked.

"I was just thinking." he replied, "I was also noticing that we have a storm moving in."

He noticed his mother had started looking past him; her gaze was set far off to the east. He turned to see what had gotten her attention. He saw a glow on the horizon that seemed to grow in brightness. It was well past dark but not by that much, but it was looking like the sun was coming up.

Dolan started to run to the barn to saddle his horse to go and see what was going on when his mother stopped him. He looked at her and for the first time he saw fear in her eyes. He had seen her worried and even grieved, but never had he seen her full of fear.

"You don't need to go there my son!" she said in a shaking voice.

"What is wrong mother?" Dolan asked.

"It appears the village is burning," was her reply through tears that were starting to form. "Quick we must get some supplies and head west into the mountains."

"But what of the livestock?" asked Dolan.

"Forget them, there is no time!" replied his mother.

They both ran into the cottage, his mother giving orders to him as they entered. They grabbed dried fruits and meats, and their warm cloaks and walking staffs. Then they headed out the back door just as the rain started to fall. It was light at first, but it didn't take long for it to start getting heavy. Lightning lit the night sky as they ran across the field.

They had just reached the trees when Dolan heard the horses in the barn calling out in terror. He glances back in time to see the barn go up in flames. His mother grabbed him and pulled him on. They were having difficulty running through the wet trees. Branches slapped them in the face. He could feel welts on his cheeks. He couldn't hear any more sounds for the sound of blood rushing through him. His chest hurt from the labored breathing. He had never had to run this hard before, but for some reason he knew his life depended on running hard.

Suddenly there was a bright flash of light and the ground shook. A large tree fell right in front of them. Dolan almost ran right into it as it fell. He couldn't see anything for a minute. When he was able to see again, he was filled with horror. On the ground in front of him was his mother. Her leg was pinned under the tree.

He rushed over to her. Her long hair was covered with mud and rain mixed with tears ran down her face. He desperately tried to lift the tree from her leg. It was too heavy and wouldn't budge.

"You must run my son," she said with pain in her voice.

"I can't leave you!" he exclaimed, "I won't leave you!"

"Don't be silly," she said calming her voice.

Dolan didn't listen. He couldn't as he was too busy looking around for something to try and pry the tree up. He found a large rock and moved it into position. He then found a stout branch that had broken off the tree when it fell, and started prying the tree up. It was working. The tree lifted slightly. He urged his mother to pull herself free. She was able to manage to free her leg just as Dolan's strength gave way.

He sat trying to regain his strength when he heard the sound of riders approaching. They were looking for them. They must have been following their footprints. Dolan's mother couldn't run. Her leg appeared to be broken. And honestly he wasn't sure he could hold up any longer either. Just when he thought he was finished, he recognized where they were. He and his father hunted these woods all the time. They had built a shelter near here that blended in with the surrounding. If you didn't know it was there, then you would walk right by and never see it. With this new hope giving him strength, he helped his mother up and half carried her off the trail.

They soon reached the shelter and Dolan laid his mother in the back of it. It wasn't much more than a hole in the side of a hill, but it was dry. He went back to make sure that the entry was secured. He then went to work on rounding up the stuff he needed to splint his mother's leg.

Her leg was swollen and the blood was coming to the surface. Dolan had broken bones in the past and knew the pain that came with them. He grieved to see his mother in this kind of pain. He gave her a stick to bite down on while he set the bone. After he had set and splinted her leg, he gave her some water and covered her over with her cloak. He was glad that his father always liked to keep some supplies in the shelter for emergencies.

He slipped back to the entrance to check on if he could see anything. The creek outside had risen to an alarming level. It wouldn't flood into the shelter. It would, however, keep anybody from approaching it. Unfortunately, it would keep them from leaving anytime soon.

It was getting colder inside their little shelter, and Dolan didn't want to risk a fire, but he had to do something or they both could freeze to death by morning. Being soaked through to the bone from the rain didn't help. So, he built a small fire near the center of the shelter and joined his mother in the back so that they could get at least a little heat from it.

Dolan sat for a long time thinking over the events that had been happening. He just couldn't grasp what he had been going through tonight. It all seemed like a bad dream. He never realized when he drifted off to sleep. All was mixed up reality and dreams seemed to flow together.

When he first realized that there was movement on the other side of the coals of the small fire he thought he was still dreaming. He jumped to his feet drawing his small hunting knife when he realized it wasn't a dream.

"Stay your hand," said a calm steady voice.

Dolan found he couldn't move. He wasn't sure why, he just couldn't move.

"Who are you?" Dolan managed to say.

"A friend," came the reply.

"I don't recognize your voice," said Dolan. He couldn't see the man's face.

"If I wasn't a friend you would have died in your sleep," said the man.

"How long have you been here?" asked Dolan

"Long enough to mend Elizabeth's leg." said the voice

"What do you mean mend her leg?" Dolan said, looking quickly towards his mother.

"Boy I grow tired of your questions," said the voice with an edge to it. "We don't have time for an inquisition. You must prepare to leave here at once."

"We can't leave!" said Dolan, nearly shouting, "The creek is up."

"It has stopped raining and the creek will be going down," said the man. "And when it does then they will be here. They know where you are. Trust me they can wait you out."

"How can I trust you when I don't even know your name?" asked Dolan.

"I am called Grendan." said the man. "Now does that change the situation you're in?"

Dolan was speechless; he had heard stories about a Wizard named Grendan. But he thought them to just be stories. Grendan had lived over 150 years ago when the wars of the nations were ongoing. But he was an old man then and this man before him didn't sound old. His voice was strong and firm.

"Listen we can sit here all night and you ponder if I am really who I say I am," said Grendan as if he was reading Dolan's mind. "But it won't solve anything. You would just be dead in the morning. There is a thick fog moving in and the water is subsiding. We can use this to our advantage and slip away unnoticed.

"But mother can't be moved." Said Dolan.

"Do you not listen boy?" asked Grendan. "I said that her leg is mended. Now wake her and get that blasted splint off her so she can move and let's get going."

Dolan seemed to know better than to ask any more questions. He turned to his mother and gently shook her. She sat up with quickly with a startled look on her face.

"What is it?" Said Elizabeth in a shaky voice.

"It's time to go Elizabeth," said Grendan in a soft voice.

"Grendan old friend," said Elizabeth with a smile coming to her face. "I was hoping you would come. I guess I can thank you for the pain being gone in my leg." She was working on removing the splint as she said this.

"And you are very welcome my dear," said Grendan. Then he added, "I must say that the fine job your boy did on setting it helped me to be able to heal it so easy."

Dolan felt a sense of pride hearing this come from Grendan, he didn't understand why he would feel this way over a complete stranger saying something like that.

"We can talk more about this stuff later," said Grendan. "Right now we need to get moving. The sun will be up soon and the fog won't last long."

"Where are we going?" asked Dolan.

"We will head South West, towards the mountains." said Grendan.

"But there isn't a pass that way," said Dolan with a bit of panic in his voice. "And if we try and go over the mountains there, they will catch up with us, or we will freeze to death. There is still snow on the tops."

"Then we will go under the mountains." said Grendan.

"UNDER THE MOUNTAINS!" Dolan said loader than he realized.

"Keep your voice down boy!" Grendan said in a low but harsh voice. "Do you want to tell the whole world? Yes, we go under the mountains. What you don't realize is that the Dwarfs live in that part of the mountain range.

"Dolan my son, Grendan knows what he is doing," Elizabeth said in a soft reassuring voice.

"I am sorry," Dolan said with embarrassment.

"For the last time though we must get going," Grendan said with a hint of irritation in his voice. "The path is long, and it will not be clear. I will explain what all is going on as we travel."

So, Dolan quickly threw dirt on the coals of the fire. And they gathered what little supplies they had and moved to the entrance.

Grendan led the way, pausing momentarily at the entrance to look around out side. They slipped out quietly. Dolan didn't even want to breath, being afraid that even the light sound of breathing might alert somebody that was near by watching for them.

The bank of the creek was slick from where it had been over the banks. It was still up quite a bit and running hard. Dolan almost fell in twice. Each time he received a stern look from Grendan who seemed to take to the path like a mountain goat takes to cliffs.

They had made it a couple of miles before the sun started getting strong enough to start burning the fog away. Dolan could make out Grendan's features better as the light grew brighter. Even though he was slightly stooped he was a tall man, probably about six three. He had shoulder length hair that was multiple shades of gray. He had a beard that was well groomed and was light gray on the sides and got darker as it grew to the middle. He was wearing a brown tunic and trousers that was made from tanned skins and a heavy woolen cloak that was a little darker brown. He wore a dark brown hat that had a large brim around it. He walked with a walking staff that was ornately carved with designs that looked strange to Dolan. It was carved from a dark wood that had been slightly polished.

Grendan picked up the pace as the morning drew on. He kept very alert of their surroundings, and brought them to a halt several times to scan the area ahead, but never for very long. Dolan's muscles were aching from all the climbing. He didn't think they ever followed a given path. The terrain was rough and hilly. They ate dried meat as they walked.

It was well past noon before they finally stopped for a short rest. They ate a meal of dried fruit and meat. Dolan jumped at every little sound. His mother hadn't spoken all day. He knew she was hurting from the loss of their home. Grendan started explaining the events that were going on.

"Since the war of the nation's it's been peaceful in Amergon," he started out. "There's been a few skirmishes here and there from leaders not agreeing with each other but for the most part it's been peaceful."

"That is until recently," he sighed. "The Quantaun nation got a new leader, or more like over lord. His name is Kryen. He is a short plump fellow that nobody thought would be any kind of threat. But he has a general named Jo-ele. He is in control of the army and some think he has high ambitions to take greater control."

He paused for a moment then continued. "He has moved across the east in rapid time. He is looking for something that he fears will stand in his way. When I heard he was heading this way I came immediately. When I saw the fire at the farm, I feared the worse had come to pass. Then I saw that they had sent out scouts and I figured they were in search of you. I was able to slip past them while they were butchering the livestock to feed the army. They kept a couple of the horses, but all the rest was butchered."

Dolan could feel a pit open up in his stomach. He had thought the livestock had burned to death in the barn and that was bad enough. But to think that the animals he had raised and cared for had been eaten by those who had taken his farm (his home) from him, and now seemed to want to take their lives, this was just too much.

Then something Grendan had said came to his mind and he had to ask. "You said that he was looking for something that stood in his way. What is he looking for?"

Grendan's face took on a look of thoughtfulness and he shook his head. "I don't know. The wizard's council is going to convene as soon as we can all get to Cameroon. We are hoping to figure it all out then."

Grendan fell silent and Dolan couldn't help but feel he was holding something back. He was about to say something when he caught site of movement off in the woods. Grendan was already on his feet with his staff raised.

Suddenly a deep voice rumbled from behind the brush. "Blast you wizard if you turn me into something unnatural, my kin will hunt you down. And besides, where would you be without my help?"

A smile crossed Grendan's face. And he called out, "Flanagan Broadhammer what do you think you are doing sneaking up on us like that? You deserve a lot worse than becoming something unnatural."

Dolan was surprised when a dwarf walked out of the brush. He stood just over four foot tall. He had long coal black hair that was pulled back and tied. His beard hung down past his waste and was tied together near the bottom. He wore heavy boots, and his black trousers were tucked into the top of them. He wore a chain mail shirt over his tunic and a steel helm on his head. He carried a large hammer strapped to his waist and a battle-axe was across his back.

Dolan could see laughter in his eyes, and he figured he was grinning, but it was hard to tell through the thick facial hair.

Flanagan walked over to a log near them and sat down. He fumbled through his pockets and pulled out a pipe and began filling it. He didn't seem to be paying any attention to the looks of horror on those around him.

"You fool!" said Grendan. "Do you want to alert every scout in the area?"

"Relax." Said Flanagan. "There isn't any soldier for miles. Oh, you had a couple that was almost here, but they had a little accident." He was grinning and patting his hammer hanging on his side.

"By the way." He added. "King Thelcor sends his regards. He got your message a couple days ago and is prepared to do what is needed. So, you say this Jo-ele is wanting to rule things huh?" He paused to light his pipe. "I have been over there listening for quite some time now, you must be slipping a bit in your old age wizard."

"And you must be a bigger fool than I realized," replied Grendan with a sharpness in his voice.

Flanagan just grinned and said, "Well Finbarden is still over two day travel from here so if you are ready I will guide you from here, not to mention protect you. But I do forget my manners." He said turning and bowing to Elizabeth. "I am Flanagan Broadhammer, cousin to King Thelcor

Ironforge of the dwarf kingdom of Finbarden. And head of the dwarf armies if I might add."

Elizabeth bowed her head curtly and replied. "Elizabeth Brekhart and this is my son Dolan."

The dwarf raised an eyebrow and turned to Grendan as if to say something. But the look the wizard gave him made his mouth snap shut. He regained his composure and set his shoulders.

"Well let's get going." He said finally.

They set off again. This time at a slower pace. But nobody spoke still. It was warmer now in this part of the day, so they had packed their cloaks away in the travel packs they had managed to leave the cottage with. The travel wasn't any easier, it was just more casual.

It was just before dark when the dwarf left and went on ahead of them. He was gone just over half an hour. When he returned, he didn't say a word, just motioned for them to follow him. He led them around the side of a hill and down into a gully. At the top end of the gully was a pile of logs that had washed down the sides of the hills during years of rainstorms. Flanagan paused for a moment and looked around. Then he stepped to the side of the pile of logs and disappeared.

Grendan motioned them forward. As Dolan got closer, he was able to see an opening behind the logs. He motioned his mother in before him. Grendan was the last to enter. This place put his little shelter to shame. In the center of the cave was a large table with lanterns on it. Flanagan had already lit these. At the far end was a fireplace in which the dwarf was building a fire.

Dolan looked at Grendan fearfully. Grendan just smiled and put a reassuring hand on his shoulder.

"The dwarf's are masters at doing anything underground," he said, "The fire may be here but the smoke won't leave the ground until miles away. And then it will not be noticeable."

Grendan pointed over to the hearth where a couple of squirrels and a rabbit lay. "Why don't you put your knife to use and clean those?" he said. "We will have a hot meal tonight."

Dolan set to cleaning the game. Flanagan finished with the fire and walked over to a pile of straw in the corner and started rummaging through it. He soon pulled out half a dozen large potatoes. Elizabeth took them from him with a smile.

"You have done enough master dwarf," she said. "Now it's my turn to contribute to tonight's meal."

"You are most kind," said the dwarf. And he turned to a hole in the wall, reaching in he pulled out a stone jug and grabbed some mugs from a shelf.

"Come boy, finish that up and have a drink with an old foolish dwarf."

A smile came across Dolan's face, but it soon vanished when his mother spoke up. "Only if he is drinking water," she said.

"Blah, water is for women and suckling's," Flanagan said.

"And my son," she replied calmly, but in a tone that said it goes no further.

Flanagan looked at Dolan and winked with a grin, but he said no more of the matter. He apparently wasn't too foolish of a dwarf. Elizabeth shook her head and turned back to her work. Dolan thought he saw a slight smile on her face.

Elizabeth peeled the potatoes into a large pot along with the squirrel and rabbit. She added some seasonings that she found on a shelf. The stew smelled so good that Dolan wondered if the scent of it might bring the soldiers in on them.

Dolan sat after dinner and listened to the dwarf talk about his adventures, battles that he had fought in. He wasn't sure how much of it was fact or how much embellishing had been done. He sat and listened for a long time it seemed, and the day's travel began to slip in on him. He found himself drifting off to sleep.

"I think you have lost your audience," he heard Elizabeth say through the haze in his head.

"So it does," said Flanagan. "I will put the lad to bed."

Dolan felt himself be lifted up and being carried. He didn't fight it. He was too tired for any fighting tonight. He just let himself go deeper into the dream world.

He found, however, that he didn't like the dream world this night. It was harsh and he could hear things behind him, but when he turned to see what was there, it vanished. He felt like he needed to run, but where could he run to. His legs ached from running. It was dark then it was light. Nothing made sense. He must stop, but if he did, he would not be able to get started again. His legs hurt so badly. All of a sudden he felt something grab his shoulder. He jumped forward to get away.

Dolan sat straight up in bed. He was sweating even though the room was cool. He looked around but nothing looked familiar. He was in a small room with cots lining the wall. There was a light coming through a doorway off to his right and he could hear voices. He slipped out of bed and went to the door. He looked out and could see his mother and the rest sitting at the table still.

"Why don't you tell him?" Flanagan was saying. "He has the right to know."

"He doesn't need to know," Elizabeth answered.

"I think he does," Flanagan returned and looked at Grendan

Grendan was shaking his head, and saying, "No, I don't think he is ready. Besides, I want to meet with the council first. This may not even be the event that was foretold."

"I will never understand a wizard's way," said Flanagan. "But a mother's way can be understood, and we will do it her way."

"We won't be doing it anybody's way if we don't get some sleep," said Grendan. "We have an early morning ahead of us. I will stand first watch."

"There's no need in anybody standing watch," said Flanagan as he got up and walked to the entry. He took hold of a large stone that was beside the door and easily moved it into the doorway. After he had secured the door he turned and walked back to the table.

"Forgive me my lady but we don't have a separate bedding room," said Flanagan. "But I could put a blanket around a bunk for you to have privacy."

"Thank you for the concern," said Elizabeth. "But I am grateful just having a bed to sleep in."

At this they started heading towards where Dolan was in the shadows. He hurried up and went back to his bed and lay with his back towards the door. Just in case they might notice he wasn't asleep.

He slept better the rest of the night without the fitful nightmares. It was early when he woke, although he wasn't sure of the time since there was no light entering into their shelter. He could see a dim light shining through the doorway. When he got up and entered the other room he noticed that the doorway was inset just beside the fireplace. It was no wonder that he hadn't seen it last night when they had first arrived. He could smell coffee brewing and he welcomed the smell. Flanagan was the only one up. He sat in a chair by the fire.

"Hullo lad." He said looking up. "You're up early. Pull up a chair and have a hot cup with me. I hope your mother won't mind this drink." He winked while taking a puff on his pipe.

Dolan smiled remembering the offer from the night before. "She won't mind plain coffee," Dolan replied.

"Good!" said Flanagan. "There's not any cream or sugar."

"I don't use them anyways," said Dolan.

They sat in silence for a period. Dolan was lost in thought and staring at his coffee cup.

"What's on your mind son?" asked Flanagan.

Dolan shook his head. "I just don't understand it all."

"Maybe I could help if I knew what you was thinking about," said Flanagan.

"Why us?" asked Dolan. "We are just farmers. So why would they be hunting us?"

"I don't think anybody can explain that," answered Flanagan. "Whether you call them an overlord or warlord, it doesn't matter. It seems all they want to do is destroy and control. Nobody can understand them. I personally think they are a few rocks shy of a cartload. But whatever causes it there is always somebody with the moral convictions to stand up for what is right. Sometimes they just don't stand up quick enough. This Jo-ele guy is probably one of the worse kind. I mean Kryen may think he is in control, but Jo-ele is running the show. And he is smart and trained in combat. The other side is the fact that he is crazy. And an intelligent crazy person is dangerous."

Dolan shook his head in agreement. "I think I understand. It can be the same way with animals. I had a horse one time that was very smart. He got into some strange weeds growing in the field and went crazy. He almost killed me before my father got to me. He told me that he was more dangerous because he had been such a smart animal."

Flanagan chuckled. "I guess you're right. Maybe craziness extends to more than just man. But at least your horse had a reason to go crazy. I am not sure what Kryen and Jo-ele's excuse is."

It wasn't long until Elizabeth came in. She looked refreshed and rested. She gratefully accepted a cup of coffee and sat down at the table. She was looking around and Dolan realized she was trying to find something.

Finally, she broke her silence. "Master dwarf, do you have any supplies here for breakfast?"

"Well now my lady, if you keep referring to me as master you're going to ruin my reputation," said Flanagan. "But I am sad to say that alas no. We do have leftovers from that wonderful meal you fixed last night though."

Elizabeth smiled. "Thank you Flanagan, and I wouldn't want to ruin things for you. I was just thinking a good breakfast would help us keep our strength for the days travel."

Flanagan sat back and took a long draw on his pipe. Then with a thoughtful look said, "We made good time yesterday, better than I expected. I suspect we will make it to Finbarden by early evening. We will be feasting tonight."

"Well, I guess we need to wake Grendan then and start preparing for the day," said Elizabeth.

Flanagan gave her a bewildered look. "But Grendan is already awake. He went out to scout ahead a bit and should be back soon. That wizard doesn't seem to like sleep much."

Flanagan hadn't much more than finished his statement when the stone moved at the door and Grendan stepped in. He didn't look a bit tired. He seemed to be full of energy. Dolan was thinking he wished he had that kind of magic in him to not grow weary. Dolan could see the first signs of daylight behind him as he entered.

"Good, you are all awake," he said. "We must be on our way soon."

They ate a quick breakfast of cold stew. Elizabeth cleaned up while the others got their packs together. Elizabeth insisted that she would not leave a place in the shape it was in. Grendan mumbled a few curses and complained they didn't have time, but she told him that she would be done before they were. And she was true to her word.

The sun wasn't very high when they walked out into the forest. They made their way down the gully and back onto somewhat flat ground. The pace was quick still and the terrain rough, but they seemed to do better after the nights rest.

It was shortly after noon when they got on a path. It was wide enough for a cart to go down, even though it didn't look like one had been down it for a long time. They had just rounded a curve in the path when Dolan's heart sank to his stomach. Three horsemen sat astride their huge warhorses. Dolan heard a noise behind him and looked back to see two more moving in to block their path.

The rider on the middle horse in front of them urged his stead forward. The others stayed behind. None of them had weapon's drawn, but had their hands at ready.

"I am Loetaun." Said the rider. "Scoutmaster for the army of Lord Jo-ele. I seem to have a couple scouts missing."

Flanagan shrugged. "Accidents seem to happen in these woods."

"I figure they do," said Loetaun. "Oh well. They were more trouble than I needed to deal with anyways. Seeing how I am looking for somebody else anyways."

"Well don't let us keep you then," said Grendan.

"You're not keeping us," said Loetaun. "In fact, you have been a great help. You brought them to me. Now I don't have to go through all the trouble of searching the rest of this valley."

"Maybe not," said Flanagan. "But you do have the trouble of getting them from us."

"I don't see your point on that," said Loetaun. "What I do see is an old man and a dwarf. And that's hardly a match for me and my men."

"It will take more than five of the likes of you to best me," said Flanagan

"Is that so?" said Loetaun. A grin crossed his lips. "Well I guess I will just have to invite the rest of my men then."

Dolan heard another sound behind them and looked back to see another dozen men riding up. They had their weapons drawn and were ready for their commander to give them a signal. Dolan thought that this was it for them. He knew Flanagan would be able to take on a few of them, and Grendan was very powerful, but he wasn't sure how they would do against so many.

All of a sudden, the two men behind Loetaun fell to the ground. Dolan saw arrows protruding from their sides. In an instant Flanagan had his hammer in hand and had knocked Loetaun from his horse. Dolan heard bones shatter as the hammer made contact.

"RUN!" Grendan shouted. "FOLLOW FLANAGAN!"

As Dolan and Elizabeth took off behind Flanagan a flash of light flared off to the side where Grendan was standing. Dolan could hear curses come from the men behind them. He heard a couple of them scream in pain, and some thumps of bodies hitting the ground. Grendan was right behind him. He could hear his hard breathing. Dolan risked a look behind him. The horsemen had started pursuing them, but they were falling from their horses.

Dolan lost his footing and fell. He looked up and didn't see Flanagan or his mother. He felt a hand grab him and pull him up and to the side. Grendan pulled him off the path and ran towards a boulder.

"KEEP UP!" He yelled.

Dolan ran as fast as he could. He was surprised that the wizard could run so fast. Grendan disappeared behind the boulder. When Dolan rounded the corner, he didn't see anybody and started to panic. A hand touched his shoulder and he spun around. It was Flanagan. He was standing in an opening in the boulder. Dolan followed him down some stairs that was carved out. Flanagan paused for just a moment to pull down a door that was carved from the stone. Dolan figured that the dwarves had probably crafted it to where it was unnoticeable from the outside.

Dolan could see light down below. Flanagan moved around him and told him to come. They descended into the tunnel. Elizabeth and Grendan were waiting at the bottom of the steps. A passage stretched out before them that was lit by torches.

Elizabeth looked at Dolan. "You're bleeding," she said.

Dolan looked down at his arm. It had a large gash on it. "It's nothing," he said. "It must have happened when I fell."

"We will mend him when we get into Finbarden," said Grendan.

"How much longer will that be?" asked Elizabeth.

"We are close now," said Grendan.

"Yes, very close," agreed Flanagan. "Come follow me. And I promise we won't run into anybody on this path."

"Good!" Said Dolan. "I don't think that I could run any more."

They started walking down the tunnel. Flanagan was telling them about Finbarden and all its glories.

CHAPTER 2
The Dwarves City

The Tunnel opened onto a large ledge. Dolan was amazed at the craftsmanship that he could see. The Dwarf city was carved out of the very stone of the mountain. Huge stone columns were placed throughout the vast city to support the mountain above. All the houses and shops were carved into the walls or floor of the chamber. And in the very center standing full height of the cavern was the dwarf's castle.

Flanagan explained that the king and his wife had only a small living quarter there. The rest of the castle was for the government to work out of. It also had schools, and training facilities for the army that also lived there while in training.

"Contrary to belief of most," Flanagan was saying, "dwarves are not born with a battle axe or hammer in their hand. Although it doesn't take them long to acquire them."

Dolan had never realized that stonework could be so beautiful. As they descended into the city, he could see the work more clearly. He was amazed at how the dwarves had worked the natural metals of the earth into their work. There were designs inlaid into the rock with gold, silver and iron.

"Why would you use all this gold and silver to decorate with?" asked Dolan. "I can understand the iron."

Flanagan looked at him and shrugged. "Why not. It's just metal. We are always digging and the mountains are full of it. We got such a surplus of the stuff, we have to do something with it. Besides why not blend the iron with it. They are all natural metals and all three must be purified with heat. To us dwarves it's all the same. Now granted when dealing with the outside world of humans, gold and silver goes a long way. But we don't need to do much dealing with the outside world. That's why so many misunderstand us. We have found ways to use the silver and crystals we find to bring sunlight into the mountain and raise gardens. I bet you didn't know that there were dwarf farmers did you?"

Dolan shook his head no. He was still looking around in awe at all he was seeing. He had never imagined such a grand city could be built underground. And for the first time, he realized that torches didn't light it. It dawned on him what Flanagan had said about bringing the sunlight into the mountain.

"It is all amazing," said Elizabeth. "Your people truly are masters of the stones."

"Each race in Amergon has their masteries," said Grendan. "The dwarves with their stonework, the elves are masters of the woods. And man has a unique way of taming animals and making good use with them. If all the races would just pull together and combine their resources, then peace would reign."

Flanagan gave the wizard an angry look.

"We have tried working with the outside world," he said. "It always seems that man wants to control everything. And if they can't control it or don't understand it then the answer is to kill it."

"I am afraid that you are right," said Grendan. "There is a great deal of mistrust between all the races."

If the discussion of mistrust continued Dolan was unaware. He was still looking around the city in awe. He had always thought that the home of the dwarves was a dark cavern in the ground that smelled of wet dirt and burning torches. He was surprised at how far off this impression was. Except for the absence of birds singing in the trees (which surprisingly there were a few growing down here, though not very big.) He didn't feel too much like he was underground. The dwarves had made sure not to take too much of that feeling away. Dwarves just weren't very comfortable out in the open air. So, you didn't feel wind blowing and even though there was light it wasn't like being out in total sunlight.

They worked their way through the streets leading towards the center of town. Flanagan would pause ever now and then to talk to a guard walking down the street. The streets were full of dwarves, men and women going in and out of shops or taverns. (More of these than anything else.) Flanagan started to divert into one himself, but Grendan reminded him they must hurry.

When they reached the center, torches were being lit. The entrance was a large arched gateway with ironwork gates. They were very ornate gates. Flanagan noticed Dolan admiring them and told him how they had been built over a thousand years ago. They walked through the gates just to see more marvels of stone and iron works.

The great entry hall was lined with alcoves and standing in each alcove was a carved statue of kings and heros from the past. Each statue wore the armor and jewels of the dwarf it represented. All in such great detail that you felt they might step out and touch you.

At the end of the great entry hall stood a pair of large stone doors. Each hung on three massive iron hinges that were trimmed in gold. Flanagan explained to Dolan how dwarves preferred stone to wood since wood would rot away, and besides there was very little wood underground. And the trees they did grow underground would never reach any size. The doors were perfectly balanced on their hinges and could be opened with just a finger.

The two dwarf guards that stood by the door when they approached looked up and nodded at Flanagan. He nodded back and said a few words to them in dwarven and they laughed and opened the doors.

"Are the dwarven soldiers always so relaxed?" Dolan asked.

"How else should they be?" asked Flanagan

"I don't know," said Dolan. "When I would go to Vangraven at the pass with my father the guards always seemed so tense."

"Well that's another difference between dwarves and humans," said Flanagan. "Humans spend so much time having to learn how to control themselves that they can't master their weapons. Where dwarves like to learn their weapons and let everything else fall into place."

They walked through the doors and into what appeared to be the throne room. There were long stone tables on each side of the room. Dwarves were seated on the opposite side of the tables facing the center of the room. At the end of the room was a shorter table with two larger chairs behind it. The king and queen were sitting in the chairs. A tall slender figure was standing in front of them. He had his hood up on his cloak and his back to them as they entered.

All the dwarves were watching them walking down the isle to the front. When they reached the front Flanagan gave a slight bow and began introducing his companions. When he had finished, he stepped aside so that they were all in clear view of the king.

"I am Thelcor King of the dwarve,." said the King. "And this is my wife Annabella."

Thelcor was a larger dwarf. Not fat by any means. He was very firm looking with the usual long hair and beard. Both were brown with a red tint to them. Annabella was a bit smaller, but just as stout looking. Her hair was an auburn color and long and braided. She had a slight beard herself.

"I would also like to introduce a new friend," said King Thelcor turning his attention to the figure to their left. "This is Princess Layanna from the elfin kingdom of Shelae."

The figure turned pulling off her hood. Dolan was in awe of her beauty. She had long golden hair laced with silver. Her thin face was smooth and gentle. She smiled and it seemed like time had stopped.

"I believe we owe you our thanks your highness," said Grendan with a slight nod of his head. "I figure it was your people that made our escape possible."

"Call it an old debt repaid Sir Grendan,." said Layanna.

"I take it you know each other then," said Thelcor.

"Yes," said Layanna. "Grendan has always been a friend to my people."

Dolan hadn't even stopped to think about their escape from the scouts. But now he was recalling the arrows that had taken out the two scouts in front of them.

"We had come to Finbarden to find out how bad the armies advance was," said Layanna. "King Thelcor informed me of the message you had sent, so I had my guard to watch the path and to give aid to your passing through. They had been watching you since you left the little gully."

"I know," said Grendan.

"You knew we were being watched and said nothing of it!" exploded Flanagan.

"Would it have changed the way we traveled?" asked Grendan.

"Well no," said Flanagan. "But a fellow needs to know stuff like that."

"Enough talk for now," said Queen Annabella. "Let us adjourn this meeting and retire to the dining hall. I am sure our guests are tired and would like to eat."

"I agree," said Thelcor. "This is all business for the morning when everybody is all rested and not fatigued with travel. Supper has been prepared. You will be joining us won't you Lady Layanna?"

"I fear I must decline," said the Elf. "Although the offer is most kind, I must rejoin my guard above ground. As you know my people do not take well to being underground."

"Very true," said Thelcor. "And on that matter, I must ask a question. It is my understanding that the elves do not wish to be buried when they die, that they prefer the fire to it. Is this true?"

"It is," said Layanna. "We feel that the fire sets our spirit free to go with the wind."

Thelcor nodded and said, "Where we dwarves think since we came from the earth we should return to it."

"If I may take my leave of you, I will let you get to your dinner," said Layanna.

"Yes, by all means," said Thelcor. "One of my men will escort you to the surface. It is easy to get turned around in the tunnels."

Layanna bowed and left the room. Thelcor made a short speech to the other dwarves gathered there and dismissed them.

"Who are all these dwarves?" Dolan asked Flanagan while the king was making his speech.

"They are the dwarven council," whispered Flanagan. If you could call it a whisper.

"I thought the king made all the decisions," said Dolan.

"He does," answered Flanagan. "They are representatives from each of the dwarf communities. Their job is to make sure what the king wants done is done."

Thelcor finished and stood up. "Come my friends, dinner is waiting. And I don't like to keep dinner waiting," he chuckled.

They fallowed Thelcor out a side door and up some stairs to the king's private dwellings. It wasn't as grand as what Dolan had seen so far. But that's not to say it wasn't extravagant. The walls were very smooth and had carving in the borders. Dolan was amazed at just how much the dwarves were master of the elements of the earth.

They reached the dining hall and Dolan began to think that maybe they were masters in the kitchen also. The table was set with several different kinds of meat. Some roasted and others baked. There were all kinds of vegetables and breads. The smell reminded Dolan just how hungry he was.

Thelcor sat at the head of the table and Annabella took her place to his right. Grendan and Flanagan took seats to his left. Elizabeth sat beside Annabella, and Dolan was able to slip over next to Flanagan.

When the meal began Dolan was able to eat his fill. He went to take a drink of his water to find that Flanagan had switched it with ale. He looked at his cup and at Flanagan who winked at him. He looked over to see his mother's reaction, but she was caught up in talking with Annabella. So, he began to drink his fill. It wasn't long before he had forgotten all about the events of the past couple of days.

Dolan didn't know how or when he got to bed. All he knew was that he was brutally awakened when his mother dropped a metal tray on the floor. Dolan sat straight up in bed and quickly wished he hadn't. It felt like his brain had stayed on the pillow. He opened his eyes and the brightness of the room burned into his head. His mother had lit every lamp in the room.

He had never seen so many lamps in one room before.

"Good morning!" she said in an unusually load voice. "I thought I might bring you breakfast this morning."

She sat a tray on the stand beside his bed. He looked at the tray and had to close his eyes. She had brought him a large breakfast that normally would have been great. Except for the sausage was dripping with grease and the eggs were running across the plate. The gravy that was on the bread had grease standing on it and was coated in black pepper. Dolan hurried from the bed and barely made it to the chamber pot before he lost what he still had in his stomach from the night before.

When he finally regained his composure, he walked back over and sat on the side of the bed, holding his head in his hands. His mother had a strange grin on her face, as she looked him over.

"I am sorry you are not feeling well this morning," she said. "But unfortunately, you must get dressed. We need to go to a meeting this morning. So, get moving and I will meet you outside."

She got up and walked to the door, bumping the metal tray on the stand by the door again and sending it to the floor with a load clang. Dolan could never remember her making so much noise before.

"Oops, sorry," she said as she walked out the door.

He could have sworn he heard her laughing as the door shut with a bang. Dolan took a moment to get himself together and found some clean clothes had been laid across the back of a chair for him. So, he got dressed and joined his mother in the hall. She didn't say a word as they went down to a sitting room.

The others had already gathered. Princess Layanna was there as well. Elizabeth sat down next to Grendan. The only other seat was between Layanna and Flanagan, so Dolan sat down. It seemed that all of them except Layanna was watching him with big grins on their faces.

Flanagan was the first to speak. "It looks like somebody really enjoyed the meal last night." Then he leaned over and whispered to Dolan. "If I were you, I would steer clear of the kitchen today. You made quit an impression on that service girl last night." He chuckled and sat back up straight.

The pit in Dolan's stomach got bigger. He couldn't help but blush even though he couldn't remember anything from the night before.

"Well then," said Thelcor. "Let's get down to business then."

"Yes, let's do," agreed Grendan. "I must travel to Cameroon for the Wizard's council meeting. I think that Elizabeth and the boy should come with me."

Thelcor shook his head. "I think they would be safer here. Nobody can reach them here."

"That may be true," said Grendan, "but I need Elizabeth to tell the council what all has been going on."

"Can't you do that?" asked Flanagan.

Grendan shrugged his shoulders. "I can only tell them what I discovered at the far eastern borders. She knows what has been going on around the valley."

"The dwarves have been watching the south end of the mountain range," said Thelcor. "I will send Flanagan with you to give a report on what's been happening there."

"But your highness," objected Flanagan. "If there is to be battle, I should be here to lead the army."

"I need somebody I can trust to be able to give the wizards a full report," said Thelcor. "There is nobody I trust more than you to do that. Besides you have trained your men well. I don't think they would dare disappoint you."

Flanagan gave way with a grunt. "I still don't like going the opposite direction from a battle."

"The battle will come to you soon enough," said Thelcor with a sigh.

"I will go to represent my people," said Layanna. "We have been watching the north range. I will send my guard home. I think the smaller the company the better."

"Agreed," said Grendan. "We already are going to have one more than expected." He gave a glance in Dolan's direction.

Dolan didn't know what he was meaning by this, and to ask meant he would have to think. The way his head was pounding he didn't want to do that either.

The rest of the morning was spent discussing what route they would take and what supplies would be needed. Runners kept coming and going, taking list of the king's orders to different parts of the city.

Servants brought sandwiches to them for lunch. Dolan still had not regained his appetite. But he ate one anyways to try and fill the empty spot in his stomach. He soon wished he hadn't.

The rest of the day went a little slower. Most of the running had been done. And they were just talking about different things. Layanna had left to send her guards home. When she returned, she had changed into an outfit that was a mixture of earth tones. It fit her slender form well. Dolan caught himself staring and had to turn his attention elsewhere.

Dolan's head was getting clearer and the queasy feeling had passed. He was grateful for this since it had been hard for him to concentrate with the fog and drums in his head. Plus, it made it easier to eat when dinner came around.

Dinner wasn't as extravagant as it had been the night before. Dolan sat on the opposite side of the table from Flanagan and checked his cup carefully before drinking it. A young dwarf maid kept looking at him and smiling. She made sure to keep checking if he needed anything. Suddenly he remembered what Flanagan had said this morning and wanted to crawl under the table.

He made it through dinner all right, and this time he could remember it. After dinner Flanagan was giving Dolan a tour of the city. He took him to an area where they were able to look out over the shops and houses. He was pointing out different things that (as he put it) only a dwarf could pick up on. When Dolan noticed he wasn't talking, He looked over to find the dwarf staring at him.

"Did you hear anything I just said?" Flanagan asked.

"What?" said Dolan. "Oh yes I did, I am sorry. I was just thinking."

"About what?" asked Flanagan.

"Well," said Dolan hesitating. "The other night at the shelter I woke up and overheard you saying that I needed to know something. What were you talking about?"

Flanagan had an irritated look on his face. "You know you shouldn't be listening on peoples talks, don't you?"

"Yes, I know," Dolan replied. "And I didn't mean to."

"Well that don't make it right," said Flanagan, the irritation lessoning.

"Keeping secrets isn't right either," returned Dolan.

"No, it's not," said Flanagan. "Neither is telling somebody else's secret. I am afraid I can't answer your question. You will have to wait and ask your mother that one."

Dolan knew better than to press the issue any further. They continued walking around the city. Flanagan would stop periodically to point different things out. He introduced Dolan to some of his friends, and had to turn a few down for drinks at the inn they were near.

They made a full circle and ended up back at the castle. When they went up to the living quarters Dolan announced he was tired and ready for bed. He had to ask for directions to his sleeping quarters since he had no recollection from the night before and this morning was still a bit foggy.

"I will show you," said the dwarf maiden that had been in the dinner hall.

"Thank you," said Dolan. He could feel the redness returning to his cheeks.

He followed her from the room. Flanagan broke into laughter as they left. This made Dolan blush even more.

"My name is Sandean," said the dwarf.

"I am Dolan," he replied.

"Yes, I know," she said smiling.

Dolan was at a loss for words. He wanted to say something more but didn't know what to say. They walked in silence down the hall. Finally, they stopped in front of a door. Sandean opened the door and stepped aside.

"Thank you," said Dolan.

"You're welcome," replied Sandean.

"Well good night," Dolan said and started to walk into the room.

Sandean put her hand on his arm. "I was hoping to get you alone," she said

Dolan felt his pulse race. He wasn't sure how he was going to handle this. He didn't want to hurt her. But he couldn't remember a thing about last night and he was afraid of what he had said and did.

Sandean could see his discomfort and took her hand away. She stepped back and lowered her head. Dolan was afraid he had done what he wanted to avoid. He stepped forward and put his hand on her shoulder.

"I didn't mean to upset you," he said.

"You didn't," she replied. "I was afraid that I had upset you."

"No not at all," he said. "It's just that, well I don't remember last night."

"I didn't figure you did," she said. "Just so you know you didn't say or do anything out of the way. But my offer still stands to go with you and serve you."

Dolan didn't know how to respond. He had never heard of anything like this. He was searching for the words to use but all he could say was, "I don't understand."

"King Thelcor gave me permission to go with you to take care of things you needed," she said.

"But that's slavery," said Dolan.

"No, it's not," said Sandean.

"To take a person from their home and make them serve you is slavery," said Dolan.

"Yes, that is slavery," said Sandean. "But I go willingly. Our tradition requires it. In order for me to take a mate I am required to work for a single male for a period of time. It is part of the way we learn to care for a husband. A slave is sold or traded. That is not what we do. It is kind of like how a knight has a squire to tend to his needs as a knight. We do not mate with the one who takes us on. We just use the opportunity to learn what it is like to care for somebody."

Dolan was understanding what she was meaning a bit more. But he still wasn't sure what to say. It dawned on him what Grendan meant this morning about having one more than planned.

"I can understand if you don't want me now," said Sandean in a low voice.

"No, it's not that at all," he said. "I just am new to all this traveling and experiencing different cultures. I have never heard of traditions like this. I would be more than happy to have you along."

"Thank you," she said, her spirits lifting. "His majesty released me into your care today. Please enter your room and I will explain more. There are too many that pass in the hall for me to go into details. Besides you're tired and don't need to be standing so long."

Dolan couldn't argue with that, so he turned and went into his room. There weren't as many lamps as he had remembered from this morning. A set of nightclothes was laid out over the back of the chair. He looked around the room and noticed something that hadn't been there this morning, he was sure of it. A small cot was set up in the corner. It had a petition setting beside it. He turned and looked at Sandean.

Sandean shrugged and said, "I told you Thelcor released me into your care. That means I have no quarters of my own. So, if I don't sleep here then I have no place to sleep. If you will change into your nightclothes I will wash and mend the ones you are wearing."

Dolan slipped behind the changing blind and changed into his nightclothes. When he stepped out, the covers on his bed had been turned down and a fresh glass of water was sitting on the stand beside the bed.

"You don't have to do all of that for me," he said.

"But it is my duty and my honor to do so," she replied.

Dolan sighed. He was wondering what he had gotten himself into. He crossed the room and crawled into bed. He had to draw the line at being tucked in. He hadn't been tucked into bed since he was very young and didn't think he needed to start that all over again.

Dolan and Sandean talked awhile longer. His eyes started growing heavy and he dozed off to sleep. He had dreams that evaded his memory. He slept hard. It was one of those hard sleeps where you feel yourself shaking but can't wake up. When he did wake the room was dark. He could hear Sandean breathing in her sleep on her cot in the corner. He lay there for a long while just thinking of all the events that had been happening since that fateful night outside his home.

After a period of laying lost in thought he drifted back off to sleep. This time it was more restful. He woke to a gentle touch on his shoulder lightly shaking him.

"Master Dolan," Sandean was saying. "It is time to get up. We must be leaving soon."

"Please don't do that," said Dolan wiping the sleep from his eyes.

"I am sorry," said Sandean. "But I didn't know any other way to wake you."

"What?" said Dolan still a little groggy. "Oh no I mean don't call me master. Just call me Dolan."

"OH! Okay." Said Sandean.

Dolan climbed out of bed and went over to the washbowl sitting on the dresser. Sandean had already poured some warm water into it. He washed his face and turned to find Sandean holding his clothes for him to change into. She must have been up most of the night washing and pressing them for him. He went behind the blind and changed into them.

After he was finished changing, they left and went down to the same room they had met in the morning before. Everybody was already gathered and preparing to eat breakfast. Dolan felt he could enjoy breakfast this morning. He sat down and turned to see where Sandean was, but she was nowhere in sight.

"You were almost too late for breakfast." Stated Flanagan. "And you even had a servant to help you."

"Yes, I think that I have more to thank you for besides the headache yesterday morning," said Dolan.

"Me!" Flanagan said with feigned shock.

"If you are going to drink with the big boys then you are going to pay the same price," his mother said giving him a look he had never seen before. He felt it best to let it drop.

After they had eaten, they all prepared to leave. Sandean had reappeared. They said their farewells to Thelcor and his wife. Then went down to the stables. There were two mules tethered to a post loaded with supplies. Dwarves won't ride horses so they had decided that they would all walk.

They made their way through, a larger tunnel than they had come in from. Sandean told Dolan that this was the main entrance and it wasn't hidden like most of the others were. When they walked out of the tunnel it took a bit for Dolan's eyes to adjust to the bright sunlight. He hadn't realized how much of a difference there was in the light in the underground city from out here. They set out west and Dolan was excited to be traveling on the other side of the mountain.

Chapter 3
The rise of an enemy

As Dolan and his companions were traveling through the tunnel headed towards Finbarden, a bloody mass lay in the path that was behind them. A horse that was dedicated to his master stood near by. After a period of time had passed, the mass moved and the horse walked over to it.

Delirious and in great pain the crumpled and beaten form of Loetaun took hold of the horses bridal and pulled himself up. The horse knelt down to help his master to mount. Loetaun sat limp in the saddle. His horse walked slowly away, heading back the way they had came.

The horse would feel Loetaun's weight shift in the saddle and would change his speed so his master would not fall. This went on for miles, until finally he reached the camp of the Quantuanian army. Here the horse was relieved of his burden as soldiers took Loetaun from his back and carried him to the healer's tent.

The healer was a wizard and he started work on healing Loetaun. He was broken up badly. His rib cage and shoulder was shattered into pieces. All the broken ribs had punctured his lungs. His heart had fragments of his rib bones embedded in it.

The wizard worked for hours trying to mend him. He worked on him until he grew too fatigued to do anymore. He left the tent to go to his cot. Upon leaving, he left instruction that he was not to be bothered. If the man took a turn for the worse then they needed to dispose of him. He wasn't sure why he had done as much as he did.

Loetaun held on through the night. He seemed to have a fire in him that refused to be extinguished. After a couple of days, his breathing eased and wasn't as raspy. After a week he opened his eyes. The fire in his soul could be seen in his eyes now. A week later he was on his feet and eating soft foods. He regained his strength quickly from that point on. He didn't have full use of his left arm but his right arm (his sword arm) was strong and just as deadly as ever.

He had but one thing on his mind now. Kill the blasted dwarf that had done this to him and left him for dead.

Chapter 4
The other side of the mountain

They set out from the gate to the world of the dwarves in a light mood. They were talking and joking around. Elizabeth would make mention of Dolan's first encounter with ale. Apparently, she had been paying attention all along but figured he needed to learn a life lesson.

They took turns leading the pack mules. That is except for Dolan, when it was his turn, Sandean was always there. She said it was her duty and wouldn't listen to any of his complaints. He had told her that he could do things for himself. But she would just turn and walk on.

The weather was nice and made travel easier. They were able to cover a lot of ground the first day. Dolan wasn't nearly as tired that night when they called a halt to the trek for the evening. They set camp, then Elizabeth and Sandean prepared the evening meal.

Dolan was expecting to hear stories of battle from Layanna. But when asked if she had any to tell, she simply told him, "There is no glory to war. All you find in war is death, destruction and hurt."

He had never stopped to think about it that way and was sorry he had asked. The rest of the conversation for the evening was light and cheerful. They finished their meal and prepared to bed down.

"Tomorrow we will be crossing the river Ackles," Grendan said as they started to slip into their bedrolls. "It will be running hard this time of the year, even at the usual crossings."

"There is a ferry just to the north of here," said Flanagan. "I think we should make for it."

"That road is well traveled," said Grendan. "I don't want to go that way unless we have to. Jo-ele will most likely have spies watching it."

Soon they all started drifting off to sleep. Layanna had taken first watch and disappeared into the woods. It was in the blink of an eye that she was gone. Dolan lay for some time watching the night sky. He was lost in thought, studying the stars. He saw several falling from the sky. He wasn't sure when she had done it, but he almost called out when he looked up and Sandean was standing over him.

"I don't mean to disturb you, but do we have to cross the river?" she asked.

Dolan looked at her with concern. He could hear fear in her voice. It took him a moment to completely realize what she had asked.

"From what I understand there is no other way," he answered. "Why, what's the matter?"

"I am afraid," she confessed. "I don't know how to swim."

"Hopefully you won't have to," he said. "But maybe if you do, we will be able to figure something out for you."

She grinned slightly, although it was a nervous grin. "I hope so," she said and went back to her bed.

Dolan wasn't sure what they would figure out, but he would try at least. He drifted off to sleep.

Morning came way to soon. He didn't want to get up, but he forced himself into a standing position. He had a knot right between his shoulders. He found the culprit that caused the problem. A small rock was barely sticking out of the ground where he had been laying.

They ate a light breakfast and got under way. There had been a heavy dew so the path had a thin coating of mud on it. It was just thick enough to stick to the bottom of their shoes. The problem was that it didn't fall off with each step so it kept getting thicker on the bottom of their shoes.

As the morning moved on, the travel got better. They reached the river Ackles by mid morning. Even Grendan agreed it was running too swift to try and swim across. They turned and headed up river to the ferry crossing.

"We will have to take measures to hide our trail after we cross," Grendan said. "Although it won't be hard for the spies to figure out where we are headed. I want to at least keep them guessing on where we are until we do get there."

"How far is it to the ferry?" asked Dolan.

"A couple hours walk," said Flanagan.

They had been walking for just over an hour when Layanna raised her hand and brought them to a stop. She was looking around smelling the air.

"What is it?" Grendan asked

"I smell smoke in the wind," she said.

"Could it be a cooking fire?" asked Elizabeth.

"No," Layanna said. "It is too strong to be a cooking fire. And it is a couple days old. I will scout ahead and see what lay's there."

With that she slipped on ahead and disappeared. They continued on, but at a slower pace. Dolan still couldn't smell any smoke. But of course he didn't have the senses that the elf had. They had gone on about twenty minutes before Layanna returned.

"The ferry house has been burned," she reported. "The ferry master and his wife are dead."

Grendan muttered a curse. Then asked, "Did you see any signs of who did it?"

"No," she said. "Whoever it was went north, probably to the next crossing. I didn't find any signs of anybody left behind."

"Well, we have no choice but to cross here," said Grendan. "That is if the ferry is still in tact."

"It is." Said Layanna.

"Lets get moving then." Said Grendan.

It didn't take long for them to reach the ferry. The small house beside the road was all but gone. The back wall was still together but had fallen and partly burnt. Dolan wondered if any part of his home remained. When they moved around to the front, Dolan stopped and felt a wave of nausea set in. He had seen his father's body after he had died of illness. But what he saw now made him want to run and hide.

The ferry master and his wife lay there. Both had been beaten and tortured apparently. The ferry master was set against a post with his hands and feet tied behind him. The post the ferry master was tied to was charred from where it had been near the fire. Arrows protruded from his chest. His wife lay in the road with her hands and feet tied to steaks at each corner her clothes were torn to shreds underneath her.

Elizabeth stepped in front of him and blocked his view. He was thankful for this. Even though it was such a horrible sight, he just couldn't look away. She led him around to the back and sat with him on a large rock. Sandean was standing a little ways off, holding onto the bridle ropes of the pack mules. She wouldn't come up near the burnt house.

Grendan and Flanagan untied the ferryman and his wife. Flanagan refused to just pass by and leave them this way. He had removed an extra blanket he had and wrapped the woman with it. Then he set himself to digging the graves.

Dolan sat with his mother, trying to get the images out of his mind. Suddenly he lifted his head and listened. He thought he could hear a faint sound, but he wasn't sure. He couldn't tell where it was coming from.

"Mother, do you hear that?" he asked in a low voice.

Elizabeth listened for a moment. She stood up and motioned for Layanna. She didn't even have to say anything to the elf. The elf heard it as she was walking over to them. Grendan and Flanagan noticed the alertness in the three and came to see what was the matter.

"It is coming from under the wall," said Layanna.

The fallen wall lay right next to the rock that Dolan and Elizabeth had been sitting on. Dolan and Flanagan started lifting the wall and moving out of the way. There was a wooden door underneath the wall.

Layanna notched an arrow while Flanagan prepared to open the door. Grendan stood with his staff at ready. The three worked as a team, as Flanagan yanked the door open. Grendan shot a flash of light from his staff down into the hole. Layanna stood ready with her bow.

Dolan heard a shrill scream come from the hole. The tension eased in the three and they relaxed. Flanagan put down the door that he had actually ripped from its hinges when he jerked it open.

"Please come out here," Grendan said in a soft voice. "We mean you no harm."

A young girl came out of the hole leading a boy a couple years younger. She was small with fiery red hair. She was covered in ash and dirt. The boy had a thick head of blond hair and a crooked nose. He also was covered in ash and dirt.

Elizabeth went to them, her motherly instinct taking over. "I am Elizabeth," she said. "What are your names?"

"Renee," said the girl in a shaking voice. "This is my brother Edward."

"I am glad to meet you," said Elizabeth. "How old are you?"

"I am fifteen," said Renee. "And Edward is ten."

"I'm eleven," insisted Edward.

"You are not," said Renee. Giving him a scolding look.

"Well ten and a half," said Edward sulking.

"This is my son Dolan," said Elizabeth. "He is seventeen."

She introduced the rest. And took them over to the river to clean them up. Working all the while to calm their fears. They had asked about their parents and she tried to explain things the best she could. She avoided any description of how they had found them.

Flanagan had finished burying them by the time Elizabeth had finished getting them cleaned up. Grendan had told Flanagan that the children didn't need to see their parents that way. Flanagan agreed whole-heartedly.

Elizabeth brought them back over with the rest of them. Their clothes were still dirty and torn, but nothing could be done about that. They stood next to their parent's grave for a moment, tears filling their eyes.

Finally Grendan spoke up. "We must cross the river before it gets dark. We will camp on the other side."

"I don't want to go," said Edward.

"You must go with us," said Elizabeth.

"I want to stay here, with mommy and daddy," Edward said through tears.

Renee knelt down beside her brother. "Mom and dad are gone," she said in a tone beyond her years.

"They will be back!" cried Edward.

"No they won't," said Renee with sadness. "They have gone far away. They want me to take care of you now."

"But I want them to come back!" said Edward.

"So do I," said Renee. She pulled her brother to her and hugged him.

Sandean joined them at the ferry barge with the pack mules. They all climbed aboard and started the exhausting pull across river. Once they had gotten across, Flanagan worked with the ropes and moved the barge to the center of the river. Then with a swing of his axe he cut the ropes and sent the barge floating down river with the current.

"Nobody will follow from that direction," he said putting his axe away.

They went a little way into the forest and turned south and left the path. When they came to a small clearing, they set up camp for the night. They just built a small fire to cook with. After dinner they sat around the fire drinking a tea that Layanna had brought. It was made from roots and other herbs. She said it would help them rest. And after the day's events they needed it. Layanna, Flanagan and Grendan didn't drink any of it since they would be standing watch during the night.

"I know this is hard," said Grendan to Renee, "but I need to know just what happened back there."

Sadness could be seen on Renee's face as she sat recalling the past events. Dolan couldn't even begin to imagine what she had gone through. He wasn't sure he even wanted to.

"It was two days ago," she began. "We were sitting at breakfast and some riders came up outside. We didn't think anything of it since people are always wanting to be taken across river. So my father went out to help them. After a few moments we heard raised voices. My mother went to the window and looked outside. I followed behind her.
One of the men had a rope around my father while another was tying him to the hitching post. Another apparently seen mother in the window and started heading for the house."

"She rushed Edward and me into the trap door in the closet. There is a board door in the hiding hole that has a tunnel going to the storm shelter so we went into the tunnel. I was so afraid. Mother wouldn't come with us. She said they had already seen her. She told me to hide there until they left. I heard the door shatter as somebody busted it in. Then I heard her scream as she was dragged outside."

"I could hear them beating and torturing my parents and I couldn't do anything to stop it. They kept asking them if a woman and boy had came this way. My father kept telling them no. But they kept on."

Renee had tears streaming down her cheeks. Dolan wanted to cry also. He knew it was him and his mother they were looking for. His heart was sick at the thought of the pain this girl and her brother were going through because of them.

Renee gave Grendan a baleful look. "I think they were enjoying it!" she cried. "I heard one of them tell the others to tie the woman down. I heard my mother screaming. She screamed for the longest time. I can't get it out of my mind. When she finally stopped screaming the one that told them to tie her down then ordered them to set the house on fire. We stayed in the tunnel as long as we could. It was getting so hot in it that we had to move to the storm shelter."

Renee couldn't go on any further. The tears in her eyes were thick. Elizabeth moved over beside her to comfort her. She turned and buried her face in Elizabeth's chest and wept. Nobody said anything for a long time. They all just sat with their heads down.

After a time Grendan spoke. "I am so sorry to have made you relive that terrible event. Let's get some rest now. We must move on at first light."

Dolan sat lost in thought while the others went to fix their beds. Grendan was still sitting with Dolan. He was watching him with concern. Dolan noticed him watching and turned to look him in the eyes.

"It was us they were looking for wasn't it?" he said. More of a statement then a question.

"Yes," said Grendan.

"Why?" asked Dolan. "For what reason are they searching for us? I know my mother is keeping something from me. What is it?"

"I am unable to answer your questions," Grendan said holding a hand up to stop Dolan from protesting, "right now. But you will know more than you want to after we get to Cameroon. Right now, we must get rest."

Grendan didn't say anything more. He just got up and walked over next to a tree and leaned against it. It wasn't long and Dolan could hear the old wizard snoring. He finally got up himself and took his bed to the other side of the campfire. All the others were in their beds already, except for Flanagan who had taken first watch. Renee was holding Edward but neither was sleeping very well. Dolan felt a deep sadness for the girl and her brother. He felt a responsibility for them also.

Dolan had an uneasy sleep that night. He kept seeing Renee's parents in his dreams. They would look at him from the positions they had been tied into. They screamed at him, "This is your fault! You put us here!" He couldn't retreat from them. The images always found him. Every place he went, every place he looked they were there, taunting him.

A voice was calling his name. At first he didn't recognize it. Then he realized it was Renee. How could he face her with what he had done to her parent's? It was because of him that she was an orphaned. He was to blame. Then he realized he wasn't dreaming anymore. She really was calling to him softly.

He opened his eyes to find hers looking at him. Her soft face shadowed with moonlight. Her hair was hanging down slightly. He couldn't help to think how beautiful she was. He wanted to cry and didn't understand why.

"You were mumbling in your sleep," she said softly.

"I am sorry I disturbed you," he replied.

"I wasn't asleep," she said. "I can't sleep, I keep seeing them."

Dolan didn't have to ask who. He knew the answer. He was seeing them too. He reached up and touched her cheek softly. He wanted to tell her how sorry he was, but he couldn't put it into words. She closed her eyes and lowered her head. They sat there for a moment not saying anything. Edward stirred and she went back and laid down next to him.

Dolan laid there awake for just a bit longer and drifted off. His sleep wasn't as disturbing now. Sandean, who had him some breakfast ready, awakened him. After they had eaten they started off again.

Edward kept wanting to run on ahead but Renee made sure he stayed with her. At one point, Grendan stopped the boy and scolded him.

"You must not make so much noise," he had told him. "We do not need to draw attention to ourselves."

After that Edward stayed right with Renee. He would glance at Grendan every now and then. But he didn't try and run ahead.

About noon they stopped and had a quick lunch. Grendan went to the top of a hill a short distance away. He stood there looking around. He wasn't there long before he returned.

"We are near the village of Hartshorne," he said. "We will be there by the evening. I do not suggest that we stay there or camp near there tonight. It would draw too much attention for a party of our size and mixture to enter town. I do, however, know a farmer a mile or two on the other side of Hartshorne that will put us up for the night."

"Good," said Elizabeth. "We could all use a good bath. And these children could use some clothes."

Renee looked down at her tattered dress. Where it had been stained and dirty before it was now torn also. A dress was no good for traveling through the woods. Edward seemed to not pay any mind to the holes in his trousers and tunic. But of course, most ten-year-old boys don't.

"We will be in Cameroon a little after noon tomorrow," Grendan said.

"How soon will the wizard council be meeting?" asked Elizabeth.

"Most of my fellow wizards should be there already," said Grendan. "But it will take some a few days more to get there. There won't be any presentations made until everybody can give the facts they have gathered to the entire council at once. Wizards hate having to repeat themselves."

"Well, I for one am ready to get it over with," said Flanagan.

Edward sat watching them intently. "I don't even know what you are talking about and I am ready to be done with it," he said shaking his head and wringing his fist.

They all laughed and started on their way again. The sun was just starting to disappear behind the tree line when they reached the little farm. Grendan brought them to a stop outside the gate to the yard.

"Hello in the house," Grendan yelled.

"State your business," came the reply from the house.

"We are travelers seeking refuge for the night," said Grendan

"I thought you said you knew this farmer," Flanagan said.

"You look more like an old wizard I knew," came the voice again.

"You still know me," said Grendan.

"I'm not sure I want to though," said the voice.

"You can't change what is already," called Grendan.

"Sadly, that is true," said the voice. "Well get on in here then. You look stupid just standing there."

Grendan smiled and opened the gate. He led them to the porch. Dolan noticed the farmer standing on the porch with a cross bow in hand.

Grendan looked at the crossbow. "You wasn't planning on using that was you?" he asked

"I should have," said the farmer.

Dolan felt uneasy. He noticed Flanagan moving his hand to his hammer. The farmer must have noticed it to. Because a big smile broke across his face.

He said, "You better get on in here you old goat. Before the master dwarf knocks me though the door. Mary Beth is in the kitchen. She won't be as easy on you for staying away so long."

Dolan felt a weight lift from him. He had seen enough killing. He was understanding what Layanna had told him that night at camp. The farmer walked into the house and they all followed.

"Mary Beth, could you come in here a moment?" the farmer called out as they all got into the house and he shut the door.

"What is it Kendar?" she asked coming into the room.

She stopped and looked around the room. Then she raised an eyebrow when she noticed Grendan standing there.

"You have some nerve," she said. "Staying away for so long. You wizards may live long lives, but we farmers don't. I would give you a piece of my mind if you didn't bring all these friends with you. And when I get to know them I still might." She smiled and gave Grendan a hug.

Grendan took a few minutes and introduced everybody. They then all found places to sit. Dolan and the rest of the younger ones sat on the hearth near the fireplace.

Mary Beth excused herself to go and fix dinner for everyone. Elizabeth offered to go and help but she wouldn't hear of it.

"Besides," she said, "Its soup for dinner and I always fix a big pot of it. We never know when we will have company."

"So what brings you around this time?" asked Kendar.

"We must go to Cameroon for council," said Grendan. "Have you heard any of the news out of the east?"

"Yes I have unfortunately," said Kendar. "Just this morning news came that the ferry master and his wife at Canton crossing had been murdered. Their children are still missing."

"Rest assured that they are safe and no longer missing," said Grendan. He motioned toward Renee and Edward."

"Thank God," said Kendar. "What happened?"

"I will explain later," said Grendan. Not wanting to go into again in front of the children.

Kendar seemed to understand and let it drop. They sat and talked for a while about different things. Dolan could tell they were avoiding talking of the crossing again. He was thinking about how crossings were usually named after the person that built it and wondered if that was Renee's and Edwards last name.

Soon dinner was ready, and they all ate. It was potatoes soup with onion's and pepper's in it. It also had meat in it. Dolan thought it tasted a lot like goat meat. Whatever kind it was, it was good. Mary Beth had brought out some fresh baked bread, There was also butter, honey and smoked cheese. Dolan was glad he would remember this meal, unlike the one that the dwarves had fixed.

After dinner Elizabeth took Renee and Edward to a back room where there was a bath. Dolan could hear Edward's complaints on bathing all the way out front. They were all sitting on the front porch enjoying the fresh air.

Grendan explained all that had been happening to them since the valley. Kendar listened intently. And was truly saddened when Grendan reached the part about the crossing. Grendan related all that Renee had told them. When he had finished all was quiet.

"Those poor kids," said Kendar finally. "They have lost everything."

"Yes they have," Grendan agreed. "I was hoping to leave them here with you."

"Normally I would agree to take them," said Kendar. "But I don't think it would be safe for them here."

"Why not?" asked Grendan.

"After hearing your story it got me to thinking," said Kendar. "If word is out that there are survivors from the crossing and that they are here. Then the ones that done the atrocity there will come looking for them. They may think they would have information on the one's they are looking for. Before they wouldn't have but now," Kendar left off with that, giving Grendan a look that let him answer the rest.

"I see what you mean," said Grendan shaking his head. "It would be safer for them and for us if we take them on to Cameroon."

Kendar shook his head yes. "We have room in the house for the ladies," he said. "There is cots in the barn that the rest of you can use."

"You are most gracious," said Grendan.

At that point Renee came out of the house. She was dressed in a pair of black trousers that was made of a heavy leather. She had a brown wool shirt on that laced across the chest. Her hair was tied back in a ponytail. Dolan found himself smiling. He looked around and found that Flanagan had noticed him looking and shook his head in approval. Dolan quickly looked away and started focusing on something else.

After they had all gotten cleaned up, at the insistence of Elizabeth, they went to their beds. Sandean refused to sleep inside. She insisted that her place was with Dolan. The barn was a large one that had several stalls. The smell of hay hung in the air. There was a small room in the back of the barn with several cots in it. They each found them a place and laid down. It didn't take Dolan long to fall asleep.

It was a couple hours after midnight when Dolan woke hearing a commotion outside. Grendan was at the door to the room and Flanagan was waking Sandean. Dolan was on his feet before he could get to him. They went over to the door where Grendan was.
"What is it?" Dolan asked.

"Rider's," said Grendan. "There are only five of them. They came up without any warning. Layanna is going to the other side. Flanagan, I need you to take Dolan and Sandean with you and go to the back of the house. Hide them in the trees. I will go in from this side. When you see my signal come around and take them by surprise. Dolan, if something happens, I want you to head directly east. You will run right into the city of Cameroon. When you get there find the head of the wizard order and tell him what happened."

Dolan nodded that he understood. Flanagan slipped them out the back and they circled around to the back of the house. He found a spot with heavy underbrush and hid Dolan and Sandean. Flanagan slipped out to the side of the house. He was about half way to the front when Dolan notice movement in the back of the house.

Suddenly Renee came running out the back door, with a man in pursuit. She was almost across the back yard when the man ran her down. Dolan could hear what the man was saying to her.

"Hear now lass," he said, "I got you now. I love a girl with a little fight in her. Your mother was sweet. And to think I missed you then. That's alright I got you now. I got to save the sweetest for desert."

Dolan felt the anger well up inside of him. He didn't think about what he was doing. He just jumped from the bushes and run his hunting knife into the man. He caught him right between the shoulder blades. The man jumped to his feet with a scream of surprise, knocking Dolan back. Dolan lost the grip on his knife and fell to the ground. The man came towards him drawing his sword. Dolan froze and couldn't move. He Heard Sandean scream behind him. All of a sudden the mans eyes went wide and he dropped to his knees, then he fell forward. Dolan could see an axe stuck in the back of the man's head.

Renee was standing behind him. "That is for my mother!" She said, her voice shaky.

Dolan got to his feet and walked over to her. She looked at him with tears in her eyes. She fell against him and buried her face into his chest. She began to weep uncontrollably.

Dolan could hear a commotion coming from the front. Then it got quiet. Soon afterwards Flanagan came around the corner. He looked down at the body laying at Dolan and Renee's feet. He walked over and pulled Dolan's knife from the man's back and cleaned it off.

"Let's go around front." He said handing Dolan his knife.

When they got to the front Kendar was moving the bodies of the other four men to the side. Two of them had arrows protruding from their chest, one was badly burned and the other you could tell that Flanagan had done away with.

"The fifth one is around back," said Flanagan. "He won't be going for help."

They all went into the house. Everybody was gathered in the sitting room. Dolan looked around the room. Furniture and other items were scattered and broken. Broken glass covered the floor. Edward was standing holding onto Elizabeth. When he saw Renee enter the room he let go and run to her.

"We must leave immediately," said Grendan as he entered the room. "I am sorry to have brought this on you my friends." He looked at Kendar and Mary Beth.

"Something like this has been a long time coming," said Kendar.

"It is not safe for you here now," said Grendan.

"No it's not," said Kendar. "We will go into town and alert the city guard. We can take refuge there."

"That will be fine against these scouts," said Grendan. "But the defenses there won't hold up against the army if it comes through. You might want to all look at going to Cameroon for refuge."

"I will strongly urge the city leaders to do that," said Kendar.

It only took moments for them to be ready to depart. Kendar and Marry Beth headed toward Hartshorne. While Dolan and his group headed east towards Cameroon.

Chapter 5
Cameroon

They traveled through the darkness. Always looking behind them to see if somebody was following. Grendan lead the group and Flanagan brought up the rear. Layanna would come and go. Dolan never knew which side she would appear on. It was always different.

The night gave way to the dawn. They never stopped. It was about an hour after dawn when Dolan noticed large buildings on the distant horizon. It was another forty minutes until they started reaching the farmlands surrounding the city. Another twenty after that they were standing at the gates.

Dolan felt tiny compared to the walls of the city. They looked to stand over fifteen stories high. There were slits scattered all over them, starting about thirty feet from the ground. The outer wall was smooth and polished. As they walked through the gates and into the city Dolan was measuring how thick the walls seemed to be. He wasn't sure of his measurements but if he was correct it was about two hundred feet thick. He had never imagined a city wall could be so huge. There was a series of gates throughout the tunnel that they walked through. Dolan couldn't imagine anybody would be able to break through the walls of this city.

The city was made up of different sections. The outer section was military. The next section was industry. Then came the markets. After that was housing and schools. Next to the center was the religious area. And in the very center was the government. Even though the city was governed by a city council comprised of people from different parts of the city, the largest building (which was also the one in the center of everything) was the wizard's council.

"It wasn't always this way here," said Grendan. "Five thousand years ago when the tower of wizardry was built, it was the only building here. Over a period of time people came from all around hoping to study in the tower. Some were admitted but most others were not. They didn't have the money or the means to travel back home so they started building around the tower. Over time the population grew so much that the wizards council decided that some organization had to be done.

If there is one thing a wizard doesn't like it's something being disorganized. It is not remembered how the city got it's name. But as it became more organized, the wizards decided to make use of those that didn't pass for wizardry and started the military section. From that the city has grown into what it is today."

When they finally reached the center of the city and the great tower of wizardry, Grendan knocked at the door. He said something that Dolan couldn't hear to the man who opened the door slightly. The man nodded and closed the door. It was a very short time later that the man returned, opening the door wide and motioned for them all to come in.

Dolan could smell the scent of old books when he walked in. Old books, ink and papers. The entry hall was amazing with large vaulted ceilings. There were large support beams every few feet. Each one carved with different designs on them. Some looked like writing, others just looked like pictures.

The man led them down the hall and into a large room. The room had a staircase in the center that went up and branched out to catwalks leading to balconies. They went up these stairs to the third level and went to the right. Dolan looked over the balcony to the floor below. It was an overwhelming sight to behold. Before long they reached an arched door and the man opened it.

"Please wait here and the lord master will be here shortly," he said

A servant came in a side door carrying a tray of drinks. Another had a tray full of fresh fruits. They sat them down on a large table at the back of the room. It was a large room with reading tables scattered around. The walls were covered with bookshelves. The servants had barely left the room when another man entered from the other side. He was an elderly man dressed in white robes that were trimmed in gold. He didn't wear any kind of hat and his hair was like silver. It was combed straight back and hung down to his mid back. He carried a staff that looked to be carved of pure ivory.

"Grendan my old friend," he said as he walked into the room. "I see you finally made it. And brought quite a group of companions with you."

"Yes my Lord Falcor," said Grendan with a slight bow. "Fate has caused my traveling company to grow."

"Ah yes," said Falcor. "Well we can't do anything about fate, now can we?" Falcor stood for a moment looking the company over. "Well since Grendan has seemed to have forgotten his manners, I am Falcor, head of the wizards council."

"Forgive me my lord," said Grendan as he began introducing his companions. Apparently Falcor already knew Elizabeth. Dolan was wondering just how many people his mother knew.

"We expect everybody to be here within the week," said Falcor.

"Has any representatives from any of the other nations come?" ask Grendan

"No," answered Falcor. "And we have sent word out to them. At least the ones who are most likely to answer."

"That is troublesome," stated Layanna. "I am surprised that the southern elves hasn't responded."

"Yes, well we haven't had any correspondence with them for some time now," said Falcor.

Layanna gave him a questionable look. She didn't have time to pursue the subject further. The man that had escorted the group to the room had come in and whispered something to Falcor.

Falcor took on a concentrated look as he listened carefully to what the man was saying to him. He nodded every now and then, and after the man finished he stood back as if waiting on a reply.

"A matter has come up that requires my attention," said Falcor. "Leaman will take you to your quarters. Grendan I will send for you later."

Leaman led them from the room. They went up another six flights of stairs and down a long corridor. Dolan couldn't get over how immense this place was. He stopped about halfway down the corridor and turned to the right. There was a door inset into the wall, he opened the door and stepped to the side.

"If there is anything that you need just pull the rope beside the door," he said. And turned and walked away.

"Now that lad will talk you to death," said Flanagan with a sarcastic tone.

They went into the room and found a large sitting area with windows overlooking the city. Off to the side was a dinning area. And along the walls on each side of the room were doors opening into sleeping rooms. There were four doors on each side.

Dolan was looking forward to some time to sit and relax. There was a light meal already set out on the table when they entered. They all took advantage of this, each one finding just what they wanted. Even Layanna found food to her liking. Elves rarely like food prepared by other races.

There was a selection of books to keep them entertained. Dolan sat reading a book about the histories of Amergon and was quite intent on his reading when he realized that Renee was sitting in a chair across from him. She had chosen a book to keep herself occupied as well. After discovering this he found his gaze kept shifting towards her.

He found it enjoyable for some reason to pay attention to the way she was sitting with her legs curled up in the chair. Or the way she trawled her hair in her fingers when she was studying something with intent. All of a sudden he realized that she was looking back at him and he quickly averted his eyes away.

It wasn't too long when Leaman came and told Grendan that Falcor required his audience. Dolan was getting up to go also, but he was informed that the invitation was for Grendan alone. So he returned to his reading. After a few hours Grendan returned. He would not go into any details of his meeting with Falcor.

"There is still much more to discuss," he said. "We will be talking again later this evening."

It was shortly after the evening meal when Leaman returned for Grendan. This time Flanagan was called for also. Dolan was on his second book by then and was too interested in it to care that he wasn't included.

He grew tired of reading after some time had passed. So he walked over and was looking out the window at the city. It was getting dark and he saw lights going on all over the city. He could make out somebody walking down each side of the streets lighting the street lamps. He was lost in thought over the spectacular sight of the city at night when he realized somebody was standing next to him. He turned to find Renee looking out over the city also.

"It's a breath taking sight isn't it?" she said.

"Yes," said Dolan. "I have never seen anything like it."

"Have you always been on a farm?" Renee asked.

"All my life," he said. "I made a few trips to Vangraven with my father, but it was a small village and didn't have any comparison to this place."

"I was always at the crossing," she said. "We never went anywhere. My father's work wouldn't let him leave."

Dolan could hear the sadness in her voice. "I am sorry," he said.

They stood looking out the window in silence. Each lost in thought.

"It's not your fault," she said in a soft voice.

"What?" Dolan said turning to her.

"My parent's death," she said. "It's not your fault."

Dolan didn't know what to say. He stood and looked at her for a long moment. He wasn't even sure if he was breathing.

"I heard you talking in your sleep the other night," she said. "And at first I wanted to blame you. But I know it wasn't your fault."

"But they were looking for me," he said.

"That may be so," she said. "But you can't control what another man does. Some men are just plain evil. They will find a reason to do things that are wrong. There is nothing anybody can do to change that. I don't know why they were searching for you. But they were and it brought them to our door. Even if you had walked right out to them, they would have still done what they did. That's what evil does. Don't blame yourself Dolan. You can't blame yourself for things you can't change."

Dolan didn't know what to say. All he could do was stand there and look into her beautiful hazel eyes. He wanted to reach out and touch her. Then she turned away and went to her room. Dolan stood there a little longer pondering what she had just said. After a few minutes he decided to go to bed.

The next morning Dolan slept in. His room was dark and nobody woke him so he wasn't sure how late it was when he finally got up and left his room. He discovered it was midmorning and everybody was already up and sitting around the common room. That is except for Grendan and Layanna this time.

Dolan spent the morning trying to keep himself occupied. He wasn't liking being cooped up. He had been pacing the floor all morning when Flanagan had apparently had his fill of it. He suggested that Dolan remove himself from the room. In a polite dwarf manner.

Dolan walked over to the door and pulled the rope. He waited for some kind of response. It seemed like ages for something to happen. Dolan started to pace again then changed his mind when he glanced over at Flanagan and saw the look on his face. He had just resolved to sit down when Leaman walked in.

"Do you require something?" Leaman asked.

"Yes," said Dolan. "Is it possible to go out to do something?"

"I will make arrangements," Leaman told him. And walked out the door.

"Would anybody else like to go with me?" He asked.

"That would be a nice change," said Renee.

Sandean and Edward agreed. They had just gotten prepared when there was a knock on the door. A young man walked in and looked around at them.

"I am Yardell," he said. "I will be your guide."

He was a tall man that looked to be in his mid-twenties. He was about six feet tall and had on light gray robes. He had brown hair that hung down just past his shoulders and a short beard. He carried a slender walking staff that didn't have any markings on it.

Dolan and his group were ready to go and followed him out the door. They all gathered in the hall and looked around taking in the surroundings. They hadn't paid any attention the day before when they had come up to their room. Dolan could understand why since the hall was just a bare hallway that didn't even have any paintings or tapestries on the walls.

"Where would you like to go?" asked Yardell.

"Any place but these rooms for a while," said Dolan.

"We have a beautiful central garden area," said Yardell.

He led them down to the staircase and they started to descend down to the main level. When they reached the bottom of the stairs he led them towards the back of the building. Dolan soon discovered that this was not the back of the building but the center.

Yardell led them through a pair of glass doors. The sight they were met with was breath taking. The scent of the grass and flowers was a welcome change from the musty book smell of the inside of the tower.

There was a stream running through the garden. It started in fountain at the center and flowed out to all four corners. The fountain was fed by artesian well. There were vines with all kinds of different colored flowers growing up the rock of the fountain, and ornately carved benches sat scattered around the garden. Birds sang in the trees. Rabbits and squirrels scurried around in the bushes. The pathway was paved with rock that sparkled in the light.

Dolan sat on one of the benches taking in all the beautiful sights of the garden. He watched Renee playing with Edward across from him on the grass. Sandean sat on the ground beside his bench. She didn't show a lot of interest in the garden. He figured that it was the dwarf in her that kept her from seeing the beauty of it. Yardell sat beside him looking about as if studying his surroundings.

"You look awfully young to be a wizard," said Dolan.

"I am an apprentice," said Yardell.

"Really," Dolan said puzzled. "How long have you been here?"

"I have only been studying for eighty five years," answered Yardell.

Dolan didn't know how to answer. He was expecting to hear three or four years but not eighty five. The man didn't look that old. Dolan became aware that he was staring and quickly turned back to watching Renee. After a few minutes he couldn't help but ask more questions.

"I hope I am not out of the way asking you some questions," said Dolan.

"Not at all," replied Yardell. "That's what I am here for."

"How old are you?" asked Dolan.

"I am one hundred and one," said Yardell. " I answered the call to wizardry at the age of sixteen."

"What does your family say about you being here?" he asked.

"I have no family," replied Yardell. "They were all killed in a fire when I was but a boy."

"Oh, I am so sorry to hear that," said Dolan.

"It is not unlike the sacrifice that any wizard makes," answered Yardell. "Wizards learn how to lengthen their lives. They are not immortal, but they do live a very long time. A wizard's family on the other hand are unable to lengthen their lives so they will die off long before the wizard does."

"I hadn't given it any thought," said Dolan.

They continued to talk for a while longer. Dolan was enjoying the learning experience that he was having. He found Yardell very interesting. He didn't look to be much older than Dolan. But as he told Dolan about the things he had done, it was clear that he was as old as he said he was.

It started getting late and Yardell took them back to their apartment. When they went in Dolan, noticed that everybody had returned. Grendan sat in a large chair near the fireplace smoking on his pipe. Layanna sat on a mat near the window looking out in some kind of meditation.

The rest of the evening was spent in lighthearted conversation. Dolan told Elizabeth about the garden and all of the wonderful sights he had seen there. It was late when things started winding down in his mind so that he started getting tired and went to bed.

The next morning it was Elizabeth that was gone with Grendan. Dolan found himself wanting to pace the floor again and pulled the rope before he gave into the urge. This time it was Yardell who responded.

"We figured you might be wanting to go walking about," said Yardell with a grin.

"Am I that predictable?" asked Dolan.

"Yes to a point," said Yardell. "What would you like to see today? Perhaps the library."

"Actually, I would love to see some of the town," said Dolan.

"I don't know if that would be a good idea," said Yardell frowning.

"Why is that?" asked Dolan.

Yardell raised an eyebrow and simply said, "Cameroon isn't the most hospitable place. Especially for strangers."

"You will be the guide though," said Dolan. "You would be able to protect us won't you?"

"Wait here a moment," said Yardell.

He turned and walked out the door. He was gone for some time and Dolan was beginning to worry that his request had been too much and that Yardell wasn't going to be allowed to take them any place.

It was about an hour later when Yardell returned. He had two armed guards with him. Dolan was surprised to see this. But Yardell explained to him that he was only permitted to take them out into the city with the guards.

They left the tower of wizardry and walked to the market area. The market was very busy with people trading and selling anything from prepared food to fresh on the hoof. There were venders for house wares and gardening. Dolan was amazed at the clothing he saw.

There were elves and dwarfs mixed in among the humans. The elves weren't really shopping since they find human crafting inferior. Dwarfs however love to trade with humans. They usually come out on the better end of the situation.

Dolan was admiring a tunic that had caught his eye. It was black leather with silver trim work. It slipped down over the head and had gold fasteners down each side. It had a belt that was sown to the back and came around and fastened in the front with an ornate buckle. He was wishing he could get it since his clothing he had was almost worn out.

It was in the middle of his wishing that he glanced around to make sure his friends didn't notice him longing for the clothing, that he saw a man standing in the shadows of an alley. He couldn't make out any details of the man, but he could tell that he was staring hard at him and wasn't concerned about being noticed.

Feeling uneasy Dolan moved on down the street to another vender's booth. This one sold knives, swords and walking sticks. He even had some swords that doubled for a walking stick.

There was one sword that looked to be really old. It was rough and rusted. It had defiantly seen its share of battles. Dolan was looking all of the items over but his attention kept going back to that one sword. The vender was sitting at the back of his booth not paying any attention to anybody walking around outside of it. It took Dolan a couple minutes to get him to look his way.

"How much for that old sword?" Dolan asked

"That old thing," said the man. "There is a story behind that old thing. I got it from a drunken dwarf who claimed it belonged to some great dwarf king that had wielded it in battle several hundred years ago. He seemed so desperate to get rid of it."

Dolan just looked at the man not showing any interest in his story. He was about to just leave and forget about it. The man must have noticed that he was losing his customer.

"I will take three gold pieces," the man said.

"For that rusted old relic?" said Dolan in with a tone of shock. "All I would give for it is five coppers."

It was the man's turn to give a shocked look. "Its worth at least two silver," he said.

Dolan knew he had the man now. If he was willing to drop from three gold to two silver so easy then he was obviously tired of having the thing laying around.

"Ten coppers and that is all I will go," said Dolan.

"One silver," was the man's return, "Or you can take your money elsewhere."

"Okay," said Dolan. "I hope you find a fool someday. But I doubt it." He turned to walk away.

"Wait!" called the man. "Thirty coppers, and I will through in the scabbard."

Dolan acted like he never even heard the man. He just kept walking.

"Okay," the man said with pain in his voice. "Ten coppers and its yours."

Dolan smiled as he stopped. He went back to the man to get his sword.

"I will tell you what I will do," Dolan said. "I will give you an extra four coppers for the scabbard."

The man agreed and Dolan walked away with his rust covered prize. Now he had to figure out how he would explain this to his mother. He wasn't sure himself why he wanted this old rusty sword so bad.

They spent the rest of the day wondering around to the parks and other parts of the inner city. It was early evening when they returned to their apartment. Dolan was preparing himself for what his mother was going to say. He was relieved that she hadn't gotten back yet and this gave him more time to prepare.

He was surprised at the reaction that Flanagan had over his find. He had never seen the dwarf so excited. Even when he was telling his battle stories and re-enacting them.

"I know the story behind this sword," said Flanagan. "I thought it was lost for- ever. Let me take it to the forge here in the tower. I will know then if this is truly the sword the man claimed it to be."

Dolan agreed. And Flanagan disappeared with the sword in hand. Of course Dolan felt this gave him time to put off telling his mother.

Several hours passed before Flanagan returned. His joy was showing in his eyes. Grendan and Elizabeth had already returned. When Flanagan produced the sword, Dolan was amazed at the way it looked. It was shining like new. There was no sign of it ever having rust or nicks on it.

Grendan had a look of awe even. "Are you sure that is the sword?" he asked Flanagan.

"Yes!" exclaimed Flanagan. Sounding like he was going to burst with joy. "It has all the markings. And the scabbard is the one made by the elves for it."

Grendan turned to Dolan. "Tell me the story of how you got this sword," he said

So Dolan set into telling Grendan all the details of his trading experience. He might have embellished a little on the price bickering.

"I wasn't sure why I wanted it," Dolan said. "I just felt I couldn't pass it up. But I couldn't see paying three gold pieces for it."

"In truth there isn't enough gold to buy this sword," said Grendan. "This is the sword known as Shoaleaqua. The dwarfs forged it over two thousand years ago. The dwarfs and the elves were close allies then. As a symbol of there friendship the elves made the scabbard for it. Each year there was a feast and the sword would pass back and forth between the dwarf king and the elf king. Each would wield it for a year showing their support for the other."

Grendan paused then started again, "That is until King Melician became the dwarf ruler. He resented the elves for some reason. He refused to turn the sword over at the feast. The relationship between the two people was never the same."

"How did the sword disappear?" asked Dolan.

"Melician was killed in battle," Flanagan took over the story. "The sword was never seen again after that. If it is true that the merchant got the sword from a dwarf then there is a story that is most likely true."

"That does seem to be the proper one," said Grendan nodding.

"What does?" asked Dolan.

Flanagan continued, "It was always thought that one of Melician's guards took it after the battle. His guards were loyal to him and would have done anything he asked, or they thought he would ask of them."

Dolan looked at Elizabeth. "Are you upset with me?" he asked.

Elizabeth smiled. "You don't even know how to use a sword," she said. "But I understand that this sword has a magic too it. How could it not to have formed such a strong bond so long ago. If it called to you then nothing could have stopped you from receiving it. Not even a protective mother."

"If you're going to carry it though you will be taught how to use it," said Flanagan. "I will start training you first thing in the morning."

"That will have to wait until later in the day," said Grendan. "He will be joining me in the morning."

"Why?" asked Dolan.

"You must tell what you know," said Grendan.

"That will take all of two seconds," said Dolan. "I don't know anything."

"You may find you know more than you think," said Grendan.

Dolan let it drop. He knew he wouldn't get out of this meeting. He went over and sat in a chair by the fire. It wasn't cold but there was a dampness in the air. He sat looking at his new sword. It was hard to believe that just hours ago it was covered in rust. Now it looked as if it had just been forged. He was amazed at the craftsmanship of the dwarf.

It wasn't in its scabbard. Layanna had that someplace working on it. The scabbard was made of wood and leather with steel and gold worked into it. She soon returned with it and Dolan discovered how breath taking the two of them together was.

He didn't want to get ready for bed tonight, but Sandean had drawn him a bath and insisted he must get some rest before his meeting in the morning.

Chapter 6
The wizards council

Sandean woke Dolan early the next morning. She left the room before he was fully awake. He climbed out of bed and washed the sleep from his face. He turned to get his clothes together to find the tunic he had been admiring the day before hanging on the changing blind.

He went into the other room still in his nightclothes. He found Sandean near the table setting a place for breakfast.

"Where are my clothes?" he asked.

"They are on the changing blind," she replied with a worried look on her face.

"Those are very nice clothes," he said, "But there not mine."

"Yes they are," she said, "I bought them for you."

Dolan started to ask why, then he felt a heavy hand on his shoulder. He turned to find Flanagan standing there looking at him with a look that frightened him.

"Since you are young and in experienced I am going to be gentle in explaining this too you," Flanagan said. "It is our custom that when you take on a charge like you have with Sandean, she will buy you gifts. If you do not except these gifts then they are not fulfilling their duties properly. It is a sign that you are unhappy with her."

Dolan didn't know what to say to this. He felt badly that he had acted the way he did. He turned to Sandean who was almost in tears.

"I am sorry," he said. "I am still unfamiliar with your customs on this. Thank you for the gift. You are fulfilling your duties well."

He turned and went back into his room to dress.

He put on the outfit and looked in the mirror. She had bought him a pair of solid black trousers to match the tunic and a cloak that fastened to it with gold clips. He stood back and admired the way the outfit looked and fit on him.

He was tall for his age standing six feet tall. He had broad shoulders that were muscled up from working on the farm. His long brown hair was combed back. He was well pleased with the look he had in his new wardrobe.

He went out into the common room and they all turned to look at him. He noticed a big smile on Renee as she looked him over.

Flanagan was giving him a critical look. "There is something missing," he said

"What do you think it is?" said Elizabeth.

"I know!" exclaimed Edward. "A brain!" This caused Edward to receive a kick from Renee.

"The boy needs but one thing to set the outfit," said Layanna.

She walked over and held out Shoaleaqua for him. He took the sword and strapped it on. It felt awkward hanging on his hip. It didn't feel heavy like he thought it would, just different.

"Do you really think he needs that right now?" asked Elizabeth.

"He needs to get use to it being there," said Flanagan.

"Yes and it won't hurt for him to have it on at our meeting today," said Grendan. "Speaking of the meeting, we must get going."

Grendan took his staff up and started for the door. Dolan fell in behind him to follow. Grendan stopped long enough to explain to Sandean that she would not be permitted to go this time. With a look of sorrow she turned back to the table and returned to her book she had been reading.

They went down to the main level and walked to the backside of the garden area. They passed several large rooms on their way. Dolan figured these to be classrooms, but he never asked. Grendan seemed to be preoccupied, lost in his thoughts.

When they reached the backside of the garden area they came to a large corridor with a set of large wooden doors at the far end of it. As they drew closer Dolan could see smaller doors built into the large ones. Guards stood on each side of these doors. When they approached the guards stopped them.

"State your business," said one of the guards.

"We are called to council with the high wizard Falcor," said Grendan.

"The boy must disarm first," said the guard.

Dolan had forgotten about the sword he was now carrying. He reached to his right side to remove the sword. The guard made a grunting sound and reached to Dolan's left side and removed the dagger on his belt.

"Take it from somebody who has been there," the guard told him. "Always remember what side you are wearing your weapon. Your life may depend on it."

Dolan started to protest but Grendan cut him short with a look that Dolan knew meant for him to be quiet. So Dolan just nodded his acknowledgement. He turned and followed Grendan through the door.

"What just happened?" he whispered to Grendan. "Why did he not take the sword?"

"He couldn't see the sword," said Grendan.

"How could that be?" said Dolan. "It was more visible than the dagger."

"It is truly the sword we thought it was," said Grendan. "The magic contained in this sword will only allow it to be seen when it wants to be seen. I must confess I had my doubts about it being the real Shoaleaqua. I could sense the magic in it, but I have seen magic infused into things before. Swords are one of the most common things that wizards will put magic into."

They walked on into the chamber. It was a very large chamber with rows of seats on each side of the isle they walked down. The seats angled up toward the ceiling but all focused on a center point at the front of the room. The center point was a large ornamented chair with three smaller ornamented chairs on each side of it.

The room was empty and barely lighted. Grendan led Dolan to a room that was hidden behind the large chair. There was one more guard there. They received the same greeting as before and Grendan gave the same reply. This time the guard knocked on the door and was soon answered by the door opening.

Leaman stood on the other side of the door and beckoned them to come in. The room was of good size. There was a large oval shaped table in the center of the room with several chairs around it. At one end was seated Falcor. Four other men sat at either side of the table.

Leaman led Dolan to the empty chair at the opposite end from Falcor. Grendan sat in a chair next to him. Nobody spoke for some time. Finally Falcor looked up from some papers he had been studying.

"We welcome you young Dolan," he said. "I am sorry to have to bring you in here for all these questions but it is of great need."

"I understand," said Dolan. "Although I must say I don't know what I can tell you. I have barely been out of the valley."

"We understand that," said Falcor. "It may not be you that gets most of the questions."

"I do not understand," said Dolan.

"It is time you were told some things of your families past," said Grendan. "It could have an impact on your future."

"How much have you been told about your family's history?" asked Falcor.

"Not much," answered Dolan. "My mother won't speak of it beyond her father being a black smith."

"What of your father's side?" asked one of the other wizards

"His family has always lived in the valley," said Dolan. "It was said one time that the valley should be named Brekhart Valley."

"Was it?" asked one wizard

"No," said Dolan. "My father went livid over the idea. That was the last time we had gone into the village."

The wizards exchanged looks. One of them looked at Falcor with concern showing.

"Do you think that could have spread?" he asked.

Falcor looked concerned. "It could have," he said. "Vangraven had a lot of strangers in it the last three years. If Kryen had a spy there then it is possible."

"What do you mean?" asked Dolan. He didn't get an answer though. The wizards started talking among themselves and seemed to be ignoring him altogether now. Dolan grew irritated and felt himself getting angry.

"WOULD SOMEBODY ANSWER ME?" Dolan screamed out jumping to his feet. Surprising all others in the room including himself.

They all sat back and looked at him a moment. He was feeling like he wanted to crawl into a hole. But his stubbornness wouldn't let him.

Falcor stood up and looked Dolan in the eyes. His gaze was cold and even. Dolan didn't know if it was bravery or the stupidity of youth that kept him standing and staring back. Or maybe just plain fear had him frozen. What ever it was he didn't move.

"It means," Falcor was saying, "that even though you didn't think you could offer anything to this meeting, you might have given us a big piece of what brought the attack about. Now sit down and take your pla…" Falcor stopped dead when he looked down and saw the sword at Dolan's waist.

"How did you slip that in here?' he demanded in an angry voice.

Grendan was on his feet before Dolan could respond. "Do you not recognize it?" he asked Falcor.

Falcor looked closely. "Could it be?" he sai,. "But how?"

"I think we all need to be seated and let Dolan explain it," said Grendan.

The edge seemed to lift a bit in the room and they sat while Dolan told his story. He didn't do any embellishing this time. He just wanted to tell it and be done. Afterwards Grendan explained that Flanagan had cleaned it and confirmed it was authentic.

Falcor looked at Dolan and sighed. "I don't know why it chose you," he said, "But it did. Zeamar here is the one to explain to you about the prophecy. So I will let him take that part."

A short balding wizard with a thick beard turned towards Dolan. He had on small-wired frame glasses that were barely held up by his short nose. He wrinkled his forehead and smiled. He almost looked half crazy when he did this.

"Well now," he began, "It was not long after the fall of Melician and the loss of the sword. The dwarves and the elves were on the brink of war. They each accused the other of taking it and hiding it. A young wizard by the name of Delcimar was in meditation and a spirit came upon him and showed him the future."

"So the saying goes," said one of the wizards.

"This is the true tell of it Sanderk," said Zeamar sharply.

"Enough!" said Falcor. "Sanderk keep your opinions to yourself. We know you have no faith in the prophecies. Please continue Zeamar."

"As I was saying," continued Zeamar, "Delcimar was shown the future. The sword would be lost to all until one of pure heart would rise to carry it. Then it would be reunited with its sister the staff of Leacor. The staff was made from the same tree that the fibers for the scabbard were made from. And the metals were forged together with the sword. It is said that the sword will lead its yielder to the staff."

"What happened to the staff?" asked Dolan.

"The staff was carried by the head of the wizards council," said Zeamar. "Kaylar was his name. And he was so distraught over all that was going on that he went into the mountains and was never seen again."

"It is kind of strange that both would disappear at the same time," said Dolan.

"My point exactly," said Sanderk. Then he sat back and said nothing more.

"Yes that is understandable," said Zeamar, "But you have to remember the mind set of the people. They thought that whoever controlled at least one of the artifacts would be able to rule over all. So Kaylar took away the temptation to fight over something else."

"Did it work?" asked Dolan.

"To a point, yes," said Zeamar. "There was no fighting. But there also was no friendship. But in the foretelling of Delcimar was hope. Because the one to wield the two together would bring peace and friendship back to the two nations. There was a draw back to this for Delcimar though. It would be one of his descendants that would bring the two together."

"Why was that a drawback?" asked Dolan.

Zeamar shrugged. "Because there were leaders of men that wanted the war between the elves and dwarfs. And they would stop at nothing, even murder to achieve this. So the wizards took Delcimar and hid him in a valley surrounded by mountains. The Valley had only one pass into it. So a village was built there to guard it."

All of a sudden it dawned on Dolan just what was being said. "My valley!" he exclaimed. "But we are the only family in the valley."

"Well he is only half dense," said a wizard that hadn't had any input so far.

"Come now Dyen," said Grendan. "It's a lot for one so young to take in."

Zeamar smiled. "Yes and that would mean that since you are the only family from the valley and you did find the sword. You are the descendant we were told about. You are a child of prophecy."

Dolan couldn't say anything. He had so much racing through his mind that he couldn't sort it all out. He was just a farm boy. Nothing more. He didn't want to be anything more.

Zeamar waited a moment for Dolan to grasp what had been said then continued. "The wizards council had a wizard to keep an eye on your family. Because of the circumstances Delcimar had to give up the life spell and live out his days as a normal man. The council controlled the marriages."

"So the council chose who my father would marry," said Dolan.

"Actually," said Zeamar. "That is the only marriage they didn't control. You see your mother was a wizard's apprentice. She was assigned to the wizard that was the protector of your father. She was young and when she went with her master to visit your father's family she fell in love with your father. Some of the council protested. But her master urged things on."

"And I was right to do so," said Grendan with a smile.

"Yes well that doesn't really matter now," said Zeamar. "What does matter now, however, is what's the next step?"

"I don't think there is any question to it," Said Grendan. "Dolan must take the sword and go in search of the staff."

"What and just let the long lost sword go off to who knows where?" yelled Dyen.

"It's what's meant to be," said Grendan.

"Say's you!" said Dyen heatedly. "I think it needs to be handed over to the council immediately."

"That's not what is meant to happen," said Grendan.

"Why not?" asked Dyen.

"The prophecy does not require it," said Grendan

"The prophecy is for a wizard, not a boy," said Dyen

"I don't recall that the prophecy said it would come to a wizard," said Grendan. "It does say it will come to the descendant of a wizard though."

"Enough of this bickering!" said Falcor. "This is going to take some deliberation and I think it would be best if the boy turns the sword over to us for now."

Grendan started to protest when Dolan stood to his feet. He had no control over his actions. He stood tall and drew the sword from it scabbard. The blade gleamed brightly in the lowly lit room.

Dolan began to speak in a voice that was not his own. "Who dares to go against that which has been foretold? I have chosen who shall be the reuniter of power. The steps have been put into motion. No man living shall change what will be. The dangers are great before you, but they are greater if you rise against me. If you wish to challenge what has been decided then you face a judgment that you can not imagine."

The light dimmed and Dolan felt himself sinking to the floor. He was able to gather himself enough to lower down into his chair. He felt flushed and drained. He could see the surprised looks on all the faces around him.

Nobody spoke for some time. They all just sat looking at each other. It was Dolan who finally broke the silence.

"What just happened?" his voice was shaky and raspy.

Grendan looked at him and forced a smile. "You my boy were just used by a spirit. He channeled his voice through you."

Dolan felt uneasy at this thought. It just wasn't natural for something like this to happen. He sat back down in his seat. He didn't even remember standing up. He was still shaking and wasn't sure how to respond.

"Well let a fellow be a little late and he almost misses out on all the fun." Came an unfamiliar voice from behind. Dolan would have bolted for the door had the voice not come from that direction. Dolan turned to see where the voice came from to see a tall figure coming out of the shadows by the door.

He was a giant of a man standing over seven feet tall. He had broad shoulders and carried a staff that looked like it could have been carved from a small tree. Dolan could tell that he was a wizard but he looked younger than any of the other wizards in the room. He had dark hair and a full beard. He had dark skin that looked tough and weathered.

"Glad you could finally join us Kelynd," said Falcor. "How much did you hear?"

"Enough to know that the boy is out of his league," said Kelynd. "And also enough to know that there isn't a thing he or any of us can do about it."

"Is that all you can say about it?" asked Grendan.

"That's not all I can say about it," answered Kelynd. "But the boy is still too young to hear the words I would have said."

"Well I don't think there is any choice about it," said Falcor. "After what we all just heard we must make preparations for the boy to go on his quest."

"It would be nice to know where his quest is headed," said Kelynd. "Who will accompany him on his journey?"

"It will be a dangerous one that is for sure," said Falcor.

"Well I will be going," said Grendan. "And I don't think his mother will let him out of her sight."

"We will meet tomorrow in the council hall," said Falcor. "I think all who has come here with him should be there."

"Good," said Kelynd. "I would request private council with you and Grendan before we all leave this evening though."

Falcor nodded his approval and closed the meeting out. He told Dolan to wait for Grendan here. Falcor, Grendan and Kelynd left the room through a door that was behind Falcor. Dolan got a glance into the room beyond before they shut the door. All Dolan could make out was a desk with a couple of chairs in front of it. He figured this was Falcor's office.

He heard voices but couldn't make out any of the words being said. A couple of times the voices were raised. He thought they sounded more surprised than angry. This went on for some time. Finally the door opened and Grendan came out. The look on his face was a mixture of anger and puzzlement.

Grendan didn't speak much on the walk back to their apartment. Dolan didn't push him to, partly out of respect. But mostly it was probably out of fear. He wasn't sure he wanted to know what was bothering the wizard. Besides he had enough to worry about himself. He was about to embark on a quest that he didn't have the slightest idea on where to go.

They reached the apartment to find that dinner had been brought. Dolan hadn't realized how hungry he was until then. He hadn't really eaten since breakfast. He sat down and was hurried back up by his mother.

"You must remember your manners and go wash up before you sit to eat," Elizabeth told him.

After putting his sword away and washing up he returned. Grendan was letting everyone know that they were all required to go to the meeting the next morning. He sat down next to Renee and began to eat. The meal was very filling and the conversation was light and uplifting. Flanagan was telling stories. Unlike his usual stories of battles, he was actually telling funny ones. Dolan noticed how well the dwarf could tell stories. He could imagine him being a storyteller.

After dinner they all retired to the sitting area. Elizabeth had prepared a big kettle of hot cider and with help from Renee and Sandean was passing out large mugs to everyone. Of course Flanagan added some kind of liquid to his that had a golden tint to it.

After the cider had all been passed out and everybody had settled down into they're chairs Layanna brought out a stringed instrument. Renee told Dolan that Layanna had made the instrument herself.

She began to play the instrument, and the music that it produced was mesmerizing. When Layanna started to sing it was breathtaking. Her voice was just as hypnotic as the music that was being played.

She sang of far away places that were lost in time. Dolan closed his eyes and could see the places she sang of. He could see the elves cities and the forest that surrounded it. He wanted to go there. He would never leave if he could just go. He saw waterfalls flowing and thundering. He could almost feel the mist hitting him in the face.

Layanna brought the song to an end. Dolan felt himself wanting to cry. He didn't want the song to end. He wanted it to continue. He wanted to stay lost in the music and the words.

He opened his eyes to find that hours had passed. It was dark out. Dolan looked around the room and could see that he wasn't the only one to get lost in the music. Nobody spoke for some time.

Renee was the one to break the silence. "That was so beautiful. I can't find words to truly describe it."

"Thank you," said Layanna. "It is the story of Sharaleah."

"What is Sharaleah?" asked Dolan

"It is where my people believe our spirit goes when we die," answered Layanna.

They all sat and spoke for a while. Nobody spoke of the upcoming meeting or what had been taking place the last few days. It was all light hearted and happy. Dolan found that he enjoyed hearing the different thoughts that they each had on what happened to a person when they died. He knew that most would find this type of talk unnerving but he wasn't bothered with it tonight.

Dolan started growing tired and excused himself from the rest of them. He went to his room and changed into his nightclothes and went to bed. He lay there thinking of all he had heard today and all that had happened. He didn't even realize when he drifted off to sleep.

When Dolan woke the next morning he found his clothes cleaned and pressed. He was afraid he was coming to expect this too much and wondered if it would be an insult to ask Sandean not to spoil him so much. Figuring it probably would be he put the idea to the back of his mind.

The common room was all a bustle with everyone getting ready to go to the meeting. Layanna, Flanagan and Grendan were the only ones not rushing around trying to prepare. Edward was running all over the place getting this or moving that for somebody. Dolan felt sorry for the boy because he knew that Edward didn't understand what all the hustling was for.

It wasn't long before there was a knock on the door. Since Dolan was the closest he answered it. On the other side was a young man that didn't look much older than Dolan. But that could be a miss giving.

Dolan had learned not to jump to conclusions on age around here.

"The council will convene in thirty minutes," he said. He then turned and ran down the corridor and was gone.

Dolan didn't even have time to say thank you. Dolan closed the door and went back to let the others know. He found this just added more running around. Elizabeth was straightening Edwards outfit and gave Dolan a smile.

Soon they were all ready. They headed out to the council hall. Renee was instructing Edward to stay sitting and quiet. She told him that if he disrupted the council it was hard to tell what they might do. They might even turn him into a frog or something. Edward got a thoughtful look on his face and Dolan figured he might be thinking of what it would be like to be a frog.

They reached the council hall and were admitted without any questions asked. When they got inside they found that the hall was very crowded. Grendan led them to the front of the crowd and into the central area before the dais that the council sat upon. There were seven chairs set up before the dais. Grendan motioned for them to be seated and he disappeared into the back chambers.

Only a short time had passed when Leaman entered from a side door. He was dressed in red robes that were trimmed in silver. He was carrying an ordinate staff of silver. It was inlaid with red stones. He raised the staff in the air and sparks flew from the end of it when he brought it back down onto the marble floor. The room got quiet instantly.

"All stand," he ordered.

The entire room stood. Nobody said a word. Dolan could hear his heart beating it was so quiet. Dolan looked up to the dais to see the wizards filling in. They were all dressed in silky white robes that were trimmed in silver and gold braids. Except for Falcor, He wore silver robes trimmed only in gold. Dolan had the feeling that all the trim was of the actual metals.

They all looked so regal standing up in front of their seats. Grendan was on Falcor's right. Dolan remembered learning all of there names the day before in his private meeting with them. On the same side as Grendan were Zeamar and Sanderk. On Falcor's left were Kelynd, Winchel and Dyen.

After the wizard council had all gotten situated Falcor gave the congregation permission to be seated and called the meeting to order. Dolan thought they would go straight into the business of the sword and the staff. But they discussed other stuff that he found it hard to keep up with. Hours seem to pass and they were discussing everything from how much rain could be expected to the problem with ants in the crops.

Finally Falcor looked towards the group seated in front of the dais. He stood up and faced all that was gathered in the council chambers. He scanned the crowd as if he was looking for somebody. After a few moments of this he seemed satisfied with what he saw.

"We must now address a subject of utmost importance." He said. "At this time I must ask that all but the most advanced wizards leave."

At this there was a lot of movement and muttering among the crowd as old and young wizards alike moved towards the doorway. Dolan was amazed to see so many leaving. He thought that all the older looking ones would have been advanced. He hadn't realized until now that there were women among them. He hadn't even considered the fact that women could be wizards also.

"Yardell, would you please stay behind?" Said Falcor to the young wizard that was heading for the door. It was more of an order than a question.

Yardell returned to his seat. He had a look of curiousness on his face. He may have been full of questions but he knew better than to ask them. He just sat quietly and waited. Dolan had a feeling that all the questions that any of them might have would be answered soon. Probably some they didn't want to hear would be answered also.

"The prophecy of Delcimar is being fulfilled, Shoaleaqua has been found," announced Falcor.

The room was filled with gasps and murmurs. Dolan heard wizards asking each other questions. One of the most asked was, "How can we be sure?"

"I hope you have proof of this," came a voice out of the crowd.

Falcor stood and looked the crowd over. His eyes seemed to settle on a spot near the back. Not far from the door. Others turned to fallow his gaze. As the wizards moved aside to give Falcor a clearer view, Dolan noticed that it was a woman that had spoken. She was tall and slender. Her hair was so dark black that the light reflecting off of it gave it a look of blue. She looked young except for her eyes. They had a look of age and wisdom to them.

Falcor's eyes narrowed, "I thought I saw you slip in Belinda. What brings you among us?"

"It is my right to be here when the council is in session," she said.

"Yes and the sword being found has nothing to do with your timing I presume," said Kelynd.

"Not at all my brothers," Belinda answered. "Besides it's not like you sent out invitations."

"You always did have a way with timing," said Grendan. "What did bring you in from your hiding hole?"

"Now now it doesn't take a lot to notice the simple signs that have been falling into place," Belinda said. "Your nice little quiet village burned to the ground while riders poor forth into a valley that doesn't have anybody in it except a widow and her spoiled brat. I figured that you would be having your little get together soon so I just waited for it."

"Have you found out what you came here for?" asked Falcor.

"Yes, I think I have most of my answers at least," she replied.

"Good," said Falcor. "Then the guards will escort you out."

"My aren't we testing in our old age," said Belinda. "I was just wanting to offer my help."

"You never helped anyone except yourself," said Dyen.

"Careful young one," said Belinda. "Just because you replaced me on the council doesn't mean you are equal to me."

"Be careful yourself Belinda," warned Falcor. "I may decide that you need to be escorted someplace other than the city gates."

"There is no need in make threats," said Belinda coolly. "I am leaving on my own accord. I have better things to do then to waste time bantering with you."

Belinda turned and walked to the door. She paused long enough to turn and look at Dolan. She smiled at him and he felt uneasy. He was relieved when the doors were closed behind her.

There were a few moments of disorder while the wizards discussed among each other what had just happened. Falcor soon brought order back to the room and continued.
He had Dolan to step forward and present the sword. Then they began to go over the best plan of action. What none of them could do though was decide what the next move should be. Nobody knew how the sword could be used to find the staff.

They adjourned the meeting that day without any progress being made. They met every day for the next week and still hadn't figured out what to do next. Dolan was worn out and all he was doing was attending the meetings. He thought about asking a question but wasn't sure what he should ask.

It was well into the second week that Dolan was just tired. He couldn't explain it any other way except just tired. He was tired of meeting, tired of listening to theories and arguments. Nothing was putting them any closer to an answer. It was after a day of meetings that he returned to their quarters in an irritable mood. He was most of all tired of being here. He wanted to roam his fields again. There he could at least have peace and quiet.

He didn't say much to anybody. He just went to bed. He was hungry but wasn't in any mood to eat. He lay there in his bed letting the darkness take him. He drifted off to sleep. It was a deep sleep that no sound could penetrate.

Chapter 7
The Dream

Dolan was moving through his dreams like smoke floating through the air. He looked down to see the city below him. He could see the lights of the streets. He could smell the cooking fires burning. The smell of fresh breads was in the air. He felt free, free from all the troubles and confusion of the last few weeks. He wanted to float away.

He felt something pulling him. He looked down to find he had his sword on. He couldn't remember if he had taken it off before he laid down or not. He knew he was dreaming, perhaps this was just part of his dream. He wasn't sure. He couldn't be sure of anything.

The tugging got stronger. He turned towards the direction he was being pulled. He was moving to the northeast. He floated over the forest. He could see roads cutting through the forest. He followed one of the roads. He saw a woman on horseback traveling. There was a man walking along beside her. Dolan couldn't make out what the man looked like. He was cloaked in shadow. But he could see the woman well. Her long dark hair was glistening in the moonlight. He looked at her face and realized it was Belinda.

She turned her head and looked at him. She looked right at him but couldn't see him. He shuddered thinking how real this all seemed. She smiled and for a moment he thought she had seen him. He wanted to run from here before she stopped him.

As if answering his plea to leave her, he moved on faster now. He moved over the waters of lakes and rivers. He could see a huge mountain before him. Its top was covered with snow. He flew towards the mountain. He could feel the cold air as he approached. He smelled the pine needles, the air was fresh and clean.

He glided to the ground near the top. He could feel the cold but it was not over whelming. Dolan looked around and saw rabbits playing in the snow. He heard a noise behind him and turned to find an old man standing there.

"Hello," the man called out.

"Hello," Dolan responded with puzzlement in his voice. "Where am I?"

"You're here with me," said the man. "Yet your also there with them."

"What do you mean?" asked Dolan.

"Well you are here with me in spirit," the man replied. "But you are there with the others in body."

"Oh okay," said Dolan as if he completely understood. When in fact he still wasn't sure. "Why am I here?"

"That is the question now isn't it?" said the man. "Man has asked that question since the beginning of time."

Dolan decided to ask a simpler question. "Who are you?"

"I am Kaylar," he answered.

"The Kaylar, the head of the wizard council Kaylar?" said Dolan amazed. "But that would mean that you are…"

Kaylar held up his hand stopping Dolan from finishing his sentence. "I really don't want to be reminded of age here. Lets just say I am old."

Dolan couldn't help but grin. Kaylar seemed to be a very likable fellow. He didn't act at all like Dolan would have imagined and old wizard to act. He smiled a lot. Dolan didn't remember ever seeing Falcor smile.

"And you won't," said Kaylar.

"I am sorry, what do you mean I won't?" asked Dolan.

"You won't see Falcor smile," said Kaylar. "He is to caught up in what is happening around him. I don't have those cares anymore. Before you start asking how I knew what you were thinking I will explain it. See you are in a place that is between the dream world and the spirit world. Here I can tell what you are thinking, and if you were here long enough you could tell my thoughts."

"Will I be?" asked Dolan

"What, here long enough?" replied Kaylar. "No, that can't be allowed. You must make a journey. You must come here in the real world."

"How do I get here?" Dolan asked.

"Weren't you paying attention when I brought you here?" said Kaylar. "Oh well that doesn't matter. You need to leave at once and travel northeast. Be careful though because it will not be an easy path. Help will come from places you don't expect. But tell no one of where you go. If any follow then it is at their own risk."

"So I should go alone then?" asked Dolan.

"That won't be possible," said Kaylar. "But the fewer the better. And I know Falcor he won't let you leave with less than an army. When you wake you will need to leave then. Your companions will be waiting for you to wake."

"I must get back then," said Dolan with urgency in his tone.

"Not so fast," said Kaylar. "You are in the dream world and time is different here. We must talk some more. I don't get much company here. Please eat with me. I know you haven't eaten today. That's how you was able to enter here."

Dolan did feel hungry, but he wasn't sure that dreaming about food would fill his stomach. But he fallowed Kaylar anyway. They went up to an opening in the side of the mountain. Dolan was expecting to enter into a cave. Instead he entered into an enormous hall. There were tapestries hanging on the wall. Each one seemed to depict something from history. There was one that a battle field with a dwarf standing on it. The dwarf had a sword held high. As Dolan looked closer he could see that it was his sword the dwarf was holding.

"These are tapestries of history," said Kaylar. "They represent all of history from the beginning of time."

"What about the ones that are covered over?" Dolan asked, pointing at a row of tapestries that seemed to be covered over with darkness.

"Those represent the history that is yet to be revealed" Answered Kaylar. "But come now the others are waiting."

"The others?" said Dolan, giving Kaylar a questioning look.

"Yes, no time now to explain," said Kaylar as he turned and walked down the hall.

Dolan fallowed. He was still looking around at all the tapestries and wondering what had not been revealed yet. He wondered if he would be able to look behind the coverings to see what lay there. He started to reach and pull one up to look. Suddenly he had a feeling of dread and thought better of it.

After a short time they reached a doorway. Kaylar opened it and stepped inside. As Dolan followed he noticed the carving on the door. There were carven head of beautiful animals that Dolan had never seen before. All of them in great detail. They looked like if you touched them you would actually feel the hair on them.

What Dolan saw when he entered the room was even more surprising. A great-carved table was in the center of the room. All kinds of foods were set on it. And seated at the end were Renee and Sandean. They looked at him and smiled when he entered.

"Isn't it wonderful?" said Renee.

Dolan was speechless. He tried to find words to say but they just wouldn't come to him. He walked over and sat down next to Renee and smiled.

"Go ahead and eat," said Kaylar. "I have lots to tell you and time is slipping away, even in the dream world."

Dolan began to eat. The food was full of flavor; he couldn't remember ever tasting anything so fresh. After they had eaten Kaylar got out a map. The map was very large and Dolan noticed that it was very detailed. He felt that if you looked close and hard you could see the individual rocks on the roadways.

"Okay here is what you need to do," said Kaylar. "When you wake up you will need to get some supplies together. Get enough for at least three days. The rest you can manage along the way. You must make haste but do it quietly. I can keep the rest of your company asleep for a while but not long. When you leave you must follow the road to the northeast. You will be able to see this peak after three days of walking so you must then make your way here. It will not be an easy journey. I can see danger ahead for you. But don't forget where you are heading to."

Dolan had forgotten they were in a dream. Every thing seemed so real. He hoped he would remember this dream, some how he had the feeling he wouldn't be able to forget it.

"Okay now I need the ladies to go ahead and return," said Kaylar. "Dolan you must remain for a bit longer."

Renee and Sandean said their goodbyes and left the room. Kaylar waited a little longer then turned to Dolan. He had very serious look on his face. His eyes showed a deep concern. He motioned for Dolan to come and sit by the fire.

"I didn't want to frighten the girls with what I have to tell you," said Kaylar. "This is not going to be easy for any of you. The path ahead of you will be filed with betrayal and death. I can't give you details. There are things that are being hidden from me. I am not sure how long your journey will take you or how far. Watch yourself and be careful who you trust."

"Does Belinda have anything to do with what is ahead of us?" asked Dolan.

"I am not sure," said Kaylar. "Why do you ask?"

"When I was on my way here I saw her and a strange man on the road," said Dolan. "I thought she saw me but I can't be sure."

"I will have to study on this a while," said Kaylar. "I will get word to you as soon as I can."

"How will you do that?" asked Dolan. "Will I come here again?"

"You will most defiantly come here again," said Kaylar. "It just won't be in a dream. That would be much too dangerous. I will get a message to you though. Now you must go back. I will see you soon."

At this Dolan started to shake and the world around him started to disappear. He struggled to focus, he could hear a whisper. Dolan closed his eyes and re-opened them. When his eyes adjusted he was looking into the face of Renee. Sandean was standing behind her.

"Were you in our dream?" Renee asked excitedly

"Do what?" said Dolan still a little disoriented.

"The dream we just had, was it really you that was in it?" she asked

"Yes." Was all he could get out.

"What does this mean?" asked Sandean in a shaking voice.

"I think it means it was real," said Dolan.

"So do we do what Kaylar said?" asked Renee.

"Do we dare not too?" asked Dolan.

"No I don't believe we should neglect what has been set before us," said Renee.

"I agree," said Dolan. "But we must hurry. It will be getting dawn soon and we need to be out of reach."

The three of them set themselves to getting ready. They packed only what they needed. Taking dried fruits, nuts and meats to last three days. Dolan was dressed in his outfit that Sandean had bought him with his sword strapped to his side. Renee had a bow and quiver of arrows. She informed Dolan that Layanna had been instructing her on the use of them for some time now.

Soon they were set and ready to go. They slipped out the door and down the hall. The tower was quiet, nobody moved around. They headed for the stairs and started down them. Dolan brought everybody to a stop when he thought he saw movement at the bottom of the stairway. When he was sure there was nobody there they continued on. They reached the bottom and headed towards the front doors.

"You won't make it that way," came a voice from behind the stairs.

Dolan spun around with his hand on the hilt of his sword. He peered into the shadows to see who had spoken. He could make out a figure but couldn't see his face. Then he noticed the staff that was partly revealed in the light.

"What are you doing Yardell?" he asked.

"I could ask you the same question," said Yardell stepping into the light.

"We are minding our own business," answered Dolan.

"I have found that business that involves sneaking around at night is usually bad business," Said Yardell.

"Look we can't go into detail." Said Renee. "And we don't have time to explain anyways."

"Well if you want to get out of here with out being caught you will have to explain." said Yardell.

"We don't have time," said Dolan half drawing his sword.

"Use your head Dolan," said Yardell. "You don't want a confrontation here. It would only draw attention to you. I tell you what I will do. I will lead you to a safe exit to the outside of the city walls and you can explain it to me. If I don't like what I hear then I will still have time to stop you before then."

Dolan's eyes narrowed as he reluctantly agreed. He started following Yardell and motioned the others to fallow. He started thinking hard of what he was going to tell the young wizard. He didn't want to lay out all the plans they had made. He also didn't want to reveal the dreams. So he thought of the best story he could and hoped he could be convincing.

"Well you heard what was said at the council meeting," he started as Yardell nodded in agreement. "Well I was laying there last night thinking about it all and I just couldn't agree that we needed to wait. So I started to slip out to see if I could find that dwarf that sold the sword in the first place. If I can find him then I might be able to track the history of the sword and find where the staff has gone to."

CHAPTER 8
Fall from Grace

Loetaun walked through the camp he still struggled with his left side but he was getting better. He could see his men standing in formation on top of the hill. There was a man on horse back riding across the front looking them over. This must have been who had been filling in for him while he was mending. Loetaun had some of the best trained men in the entire military. Whoever this was that was overseeing them in his absence had better not messed that up.

He was about to start up the hill when movement in the tent he was passing caught his attention. It was a tall slender Man that motioned for him to come there. As he drew closer he recognized him. His old friend Kieser. He quickly disappeared into the tent when he saw Loetaun had started that direction. This wasn't uncommon for him to do since he was a trained assassin and the best there was. He started out under Loetaun's cammand when Loetaun was first promoted and even though he was his cammanding officer, Loetaun took a liking to him and befriended him.

It took a moment for Loetaun's eyes to adjust when he entered the tent and he didn't see Kieser, then he felt something cold against his neck and he relized that Kieser was here on business. But why?

"So, you are here to kill me," said Loetaun. It was more of a statement then a question.

"Yes," came the reply in a calm smooth voice.

" Why am I to be done away with?" asked Loetaun.

"You have fallen out of favor with Lord Jo-Ele," answered Kieser

"But not with you," Loetaun's voice was calm

"What makes you say that?"asked Kieser

"Because I know you, you could have killed me without anybody knowing you were in camp. Even me," said Loetaun

Loetaun could feel the blade moving away from him. He turned to look Kieser in the eye's. There was no way an ordinary person could read his face but Loetaun wasn't an ordinary person when it came to Kieser. He had fought with this man, stood back to back with him in fierce battle. He knew every little motion he made and the meaning behind it.

"So, tell me what is going on," he said to Kieser

"You have been declared a liability," said Kieser. " You are damaged and Lord Jo-Ele said there is no place in the perfect world for anybody that is damaged. So, he wants you removed before the damage spreads."

"So, he sent you to kill me?" asked Loetaun

"No," replied Kieser. "He was also upset with the wizard that pulled you through. I have already taken care of him. It is not I that am supposed retire you. That is Skyreals place. Thats why I called you in here, to warn you. The man that is taking your place was ordered to kill you in front of your men so they could see what failure in battle would bring them."

"I have heard of this Skyreal," said Loetaun, "They say he is ruthless."

"He is," said Kieser. " He killed his own brother because he mocked Lord Jo-Ele."

"I could still beat him in fair battle!" stated Loetaun.

" The problem is he doesn't fight fair," said Kieser. "That is why you must get away from here. I took the liberty of saddling your horse for you and hiding him in the woods. I will take you to him and then I must leave you. I don't want to know where you go because I will be the one sent to find you, so the less I know the better"

"I understand my friend, I don't even know where I am going myself," said Loetaun

"Take some more advice from an old friend," said Kieser in a flat voice and looking Loetaun straight in the eyes. "Don't go seeking the dwarf for revenge. I can find you that way, and if I find you I will have to kill you. That is my duty."

Loetaun nodded in understanding all the time thinking that the only thing that made Skyreal more ruthless was that he wouldn't have warned any friend no matter how close they were.

The two men slipped out the back of the tent and made their way down the opposite direction from the training ground. It was midmorning and about time for the morning exercises to be over, so they didn't take any chances. When they got to where Loetauns horse was tied Loetaun turned to say something to Kieser but he wasn't to be found.

"Well Blaze I guess were on our own old boy," Loetaun told his horse " Well we better get moving."

He mounted up and started off winding through the forest, paying close attention to his surroundings. He wasn't accustomed to looking over his shoulder. This was a new experience for him. Blaze was his only true friend. He remembered when he had found him. He was all legs and stumbling around. He took him and started training. They grew closer as he grew and became as one in battle, it was like Blaze could read his thoughts and moved with them.

People often wondered why he had named him Blaze since he was solid black. You had to look really close or see it in the right light but he had a spot on his forehead shaped like a flame that was so deep black it had a blue tint to it. His main was the same way so it looked like a flowing black blaze.

Blaze had his own armor that included leg pieces that went to the edge of his hooves where they were sharpened like a sword and he knew how to use them and had many times in battle. When he would charge into the oncoming armies he was as deadly as any soldier was if not more deadly.

It was getting late now, but he didn't want to stop. He wasn't far enough away yet. He continued to ride on into the night. He dozed a few times in the saddle, something he had learned how to do a long time ago on long rides when the company couldn't stop. He trusted Blaze to find his way, but he knew they would have to stop sometime, because even Blaze would need to rest.

He found a spot a few hundred yards off the trail that had a surrounding of boulders, that he set up camp. Normally he would have taken Blaze's saddle off and rubbed him down, but this wasn't normal. So, he tethered him next to a large bolder promising him a better night tomorrow and leaned against another bolder and dozed off.

He didn't sleep because sleeping could cost him his life. He pondered what he was going to do and decided to make for an old friend's house. Kaylen would at least be able to help him with different clothes and gear for Blaze. The military gear would really stick out and that's the last thing he wanted right now.

It was just before daylight when he climbed into the saddle again and started off. He figured he would make it to Kaylen's place by noon and maybe be able to get some rest. He knew he couldn't stay there very long because it would put Kaylen and his family in danger. And he had lost enough friends and it had all been because of a no good dwarf. He may not be able to get his revenge right now, but the day would come when he would set things right.

it was about mid-morning when he started to feel the pains of hunger hitting him and he realized he hadn't eaten since breakfast yesterday morning. But he had to keep going. He would eat when he reached his destination. It was just past noon when he topped the hill above his destination, and he stopped in horror.

He was looking upon the remains of Kaylen's home, it was nothing but ash save for a few charred boards scattered about. First thing that came to his mind was this happened because of him. But as he drew closer, he realized these ruins were several days old. Kaylen had been the ferry master at this crossing ever since he could remember and to see it like this cut to the bone.

He came across two graves and from the looks of them they were for somebody fully grown. So hopefully the children are ok. He scanned the area further and found arrows with blood stains on them. He recognized the arrows as ones used by the scouts, his scouts. In all his years commanding the scouts they had never used violence like this to accomplish anything. He had found more effective means to get information.

He looked around for signs of what had happened but since it had been several days there wasn't much to see. the ferry had been cut lose and set adrift, but the river was calm enough he figured he and Blaze could cross as long as he pulled Blaze's armor off which he needed to do anyways.

There was a small stable still standing that had riding tac in it and some old clothes, so he and Blaze both took on a new look. He took all of the armor and laid it on a large tarp that he then tied the corners together on. Blaze could have swam across here easy enough but he wanted a little less likely place to cross over at so he loaded his bundle of armor onto Blaze's back and walked him upstream a good distance where the river bank was covered with brush. On the upper side of the brush he pulled the armor off Blazes back and tying a rope onto it eased it off into the edge of the water. He tied the other end of the rope onto the old saddle that Blaze now wore and climbed into it himself.

Blaze, knowing what was expected of him, moved towards the water and started across the river. He was pulling the armor behind him with ease. It didn't take long before they were in water that would have been feet above their heads if they were touching bottom. It was at this time when Loetaun cut the rope from the saddle and let the armor sink to the bottom.

"There, they shouldn't be able to find it there," he told Blaze.

After they reached the other side, they rested for a time, making sure to stay out of sight from the opposite shore. It was starting to get late in the evening when Loetaun started moving away from the river. He went several miles and then decided to set up camp. Tonight he risked a small fire and sat gazing into it.

"Well Blaze my friend, tomorrow we go find the kids, I want answers." he said and then he drifted off to sleep.

CHAPTER 9

THE QUEST BEGINS

Yardell led them to the back of the stairway where there was a closet. When he opened the door it looked like a regular broom closet, but when Yardell spoke a word under his breath that Dolan could not understand the floor opened to reveal a stairway leading down into a tunnel. Dolan followed Yardell down the stairs. He guessed Yardell had believed him since he was leading them without any further questions.

They had walked through the tunnel for a good distance without any turns when they came upon an old wooden door. There hadn't been any conversation as they walked, and Dolan was glad of it he didn't feel like talking his mind was still trying to wrap itself around the dream. Yardell stopped and reached for the door handle but didn't open the door instead he turned to Dolan and looked him in the eyes.

"I don't know why you found it necessary to lie to me but before I open the door, I think I am owed the truth," said Yardell

Dolan wasn't sure how to answer him but knew he couldn't lie to him again. He stood there a moment thinking it over on how to continue. Then finally gave in and explained everything to Yardell.

"That changes everything then," said Yardell

"Does that mean you're not going to help then?" asked Renee

"No," answered Yardell, "It means I am going with you."

"But you weren't summoned," said Dolan

"Maybe not," said Yardell, "But from my stand point you are going to be dealing with wizardry and I am the most trained one of us here, so I am going."

Dolan knew he couldn't argue with that, so he reluctantly agreed. Yardell then opened the door and they stepped out of a shed built into the side of a hill next to the outer wall. Not far from them was a wooden door built into the wall. He knocked on the door hesitated and knocked again. After a moment a small light showed through an opening in the door and then the door opened and a guard stepped out.

He was a tall stout looking man that has a long mustache. Yardell spoke to him quietly then motioned for the group to join them. They hurried into the little door, it was a small hallway built into the wall. Even though from the outside it looked like a solid wall surounding the city it actually had military barrecks built into them.

"This is Drake," Yardell said and then introduced his companions to Drake. "We must reach the outside of the wall to the north east Drake but is must be in silence that we leave."

Drake raised an eyebrow. "Why are you sneaking around? I don't like it."

"It is of the utmost importance that we do this without hinderance. I haven't ever done anything to cause alarm before," stated Yardell

"You never wanted to leave the wall before," said Drake

"I have never had the right incentive before,"

responded Yardell

Drake gave a questioning look but nodded in agreement then turned and started leading the way. They traveled only a few feet before they came to a door that opened into an even smaller hall. To their left they had to walk in single file. This was much further of a walk and Dolan didn't think it was a straight path, but he couldn't be sure since the only light was from a torch that Drake was holding.

After a while they came to an open area and Dolan could make out a small table with a lamp on it and a couple of chairs. There was three other doorways and Drake led them to the first one on the right. They only traveled a short distance down this hallway before turning left again. Dolan hadn't thought the tunnel could get any tighter, but he was wrong. He could tell that it was getting hard for Drake to walk through here. Then suddenly the big man was gone and only Yardell was in front of him.

Yardell was holding his staff out in front of him and the tip of it glowed with a faint blueish light. They continued to move forward, and Dolan reached to steady himself on the wall only to put his hand on the cold feel of metal, he almost yelled out when he felt a firm hand grasp over his mouth and heard Drakes voice whisper, "Careful or you will give yourself away. You continue without me from here."

It was then that Dolan realized drake had slipped into an area cut out in the wall just big enough for a man to stand in. He had apparently extinguished his light in order to keep from interfering with their sight.

They traveled for sometime longer. The passage got to where they had to turn sideways to get through. This made it hard to get their packs through but somehow they managed. The walls changed from hewn and laid stone to natural rock walls. Finally, Dolan could see a little bit of light up ahead. Yardell had apparently noticed it because he put out the glow of his staff. it was just a few minutes and they could feel the cool night air coming to great them and moments later they were slipping out of a small crevice in the side of a hill.

"Where are we?" asked Dolan.

"We are several miles from Camaroon," said Yardell. "We came down tunnels that were designed for sending spies and messengers out of if the city was under siege."

"Couldn't that work both ways?" asked Renee.

"No," replied Yardell, "Because even if the passage was found, a man in full armor couldn't get through and there is always a guard on duty. We were lucky that Drake was the one on duty tonight."

"Well, I don't think we have time to rest," said Dolan. "We need to put a lot more distance between us and the city. Everybody will be getting around soon and I don't want a search party catching up with us."

They made their way down the hill and crossed over a small stream, They were surrounded by woods and it took Dolan a moment to get his bearings. All he knew was they were supposed to head to the northeast but other than that he had no idea where he was going.

It was about mid-day when they came to the end of the woods to the beginnings of the plains lands. He could see the mountains beyond and the dream started coming back to him. He knew they had to cross the plains and head for the mountains.

The sun felt good and welcoming, he still felt a chill from traveling all night in the tunnels. He was starting to feel the fatigue setting in from not sleeping. They sat for a moment to eat a quick bite before they continued.

Nobody talked, they were all tired, but they knew they couldn't stop to rest now, so they ate quickly and started the long trek across the grassy plains. The young green grass that was just starting to grow after the long winter was soft under their feet, but it didn't supply any cover for them and they could be spotted from miles away. They kept watching for any sign of being followed but so far it was all clear. Dolan didn't know what he would do if they were caught but he knew he didn't want to face his mother.

They had traveled all afternoon without seeing anything other than a few birds and a couple of rabbits. They had lost sight of the woods hours ago and didn't feel the need to keep silent anymore. Although they did speak softly.

They didn't talk about anything in particular. Mainly about their home. Dolan told about how most of his learning came from doing farm work all day and his mother would teach him to read and write at night although he never understood why he had to learn such things.

He told his mother this on one occasions and she just smiled at him and told him that one never knew where life might take them. Now he was understanding what she meant by that. Until now he had never thought of leaving the valley he had always known as home.

Renee had grown up with being taught about the different cultures. Living at a crossing house they had many different types of people that came through, she had picked up bits and pieces of different languages. There were some words she didn't understand that when she asked her parents about them they would respond with "There are words in all languages that a lady does not need to know the meaning of."

Dolan could see the pain in her eyes when she talked of her parents. He had never known how that pain felt. Even though it hurt to lose his father, that was a natural death that most likely couldn't be avoided. Renees' parents death was something from pure hate and ignorance.

Yardell didn't speak of his youth, he just said, "That was a long time ago and a lot has happened since then"

Sandean Told stories of playing in the caverns of the Dwarf city and how she collected little trinkets of different stones. She always likes the glittery ones that made the light change when it shined through them.

It was starting to get dark and everyone was feeling the last 24 hours to the point it was getting hard to walk and stay awake. They didn't want to build a fire and draw any attention to themselves, besides there wasn't anything around to burn. So they laid down on the soft grass and looked out into the clear sky. The stars shined brightly and it looked so vast, like you could get lost in the darkness.

Renee broke the silence "Do you ever wonder if there is life out in the stars?" She asked

Dolan's gaze deepened like he was looking to see if he could see anything. He didn't know why. Finally he shook his head. "What kind of life could be out there?" He finally answered,

"I don't know," said Renee, "But why would there only be life here. I mean we have life in the waters and all across the land and birds in the sky. Do you think it's possible to have some other kind of life beyond what we see."

"I never thought about it," he replied, "But if there is, do we really want to know? I mean I have delt with some of the life we have on land and in the water and there are some things that scare me with that."

They fell silent again and Dolan lay looking into the sky, this time with a different set of thoughts than before. He didn't realize when he had drifted off to sleep but he was sleeping hard when he was woke by Renee' scream.

It was dark still and all he could see was the dark forms of his companions moving around. He could see four forms over from him then he realized he should only be seeing three.

Yardell spoke a word and the end of his staff came to life with light. Dolan was starting to draw his sword then he noticed a small form hunkered down on the ground beside Renee. He realized he knew this form. It was Edward!

"Edward!" exclaimed Renee, "What are you doing here?"

"You left me," said Edward holding back tears

"You needed to stay behind, It's too dangerous where we are going," Renee told him

"I don't car," said Edward

"I do care!" said Renee starting to lose her temper

"But your all I have!" said Edward breaking

into tears. "I don't want you to leave me like mommy and daddy did!"

Renee's temper left and she pulled the boy to her and started crying with him. They both sat and wept together, all of them were quiet. What could be said. Dolan didn't think either had really been able to cry and let it all out since that night at the crossing.

"I'm not going to leave you." Renee told him softly.

"How did you get here?" Dolan asked

"I followed you," said Edward wiping his face

"But you were asleep when I checked on you before we left," said Renee

"Naw," said Edward. "Just pretenden. I do that when people don't want to tell me anything."

"But how did you get through the tunnel and past Drake?" asked Yardell

"I can see in the dark really good." Edward replied. "And big people are always looking up and don't notice us small ones unless they trip over us."

"So, you have been behind us all this time."

said Dolan. "Why did you wait until now to let us know you were here?"

"I got cold and hungry," said Edward.

"Of course, you must be starving," said Renee getting him some of the dried meats from her pouch

They then settled down and started getting comfortable so they could finish getting some rest. Edward curled up next to Renee under her blanket and fell right to sleep. Dolan lay awake a little while longer thinking how lucky Renee and Edward was to have each other. He didn't remember what his last thoughts were before the darkness of sleep overtook him.

CHAPTER 10

A DIFFERENT PATH

Elizabeth woke late. She was quite surprised that she had slept in. She had never done that before. She went into the common room to discover she wasn't the only one to sleep in. All the others were just starting to gather as well so she didn't feel so bad about it, but she would make sure it didn't happen again.

She noticed Dolan and Renee weren't up yet but figured there wasn't any reason to disturb them. She poured her a cup of coffee and sat by the window looking out over the city. It wasn't as nice as sitting on the front porch of her little cottage, but it still had a certain beauty to it.

She looked over at Grendan who was sitting

back half puffing on a pipe. She loved the cherry smell of his pipe even though she couldn't imagine how someone would like the taste of a pipe. But he apparently wasn't tasting it much, he seemed to be deep in thought and not paying any attention to what was going on around him.

Suddenly he jumped straight to his feet startling everyone in the room. He rushed across the room without saying a word and went to the door of Dolans bed chambers. Without hesitation he burst through the door. Elizabeth was right behind him wondering what was going on.

When she entered the room Grendan was standing in the middle of the room looking at the bed. Then she realized he was looking at an empty bed. Sandeans cot was also empty. She ran down the hall to Renee and Edwards chamber to find both of their beds empty also.

She rushed to the common room. "Where could They be?" she said frantically. "They wouldn't just leave out without us knowing. Nor would they be summoned by their self"

"But they were summoned," said Grendan, "By the highest wizard."

"Why would Falcor call them without us knowing?" asked Elizabeth.

"It wasn't Falcor," said Grendan, "It was Kaylar."

"Kaylar disappeared ages ago," said Flanagan, "The chances of him being alive are nonexistent."

"Just like the chances of a lost sword being in a street market?" Grendan said looking at Flanagan with a look that let them know it was more of a statement than a question.

Elizabeth started rushing around to get dressed and get things together. She was starting to bark out orders when Grendan stepped in front of her.

"Get out of my way!" she screamed at him. "We have to get moving so we can find them."

"Where do you plan on looking?" he asked in a calm voice.

"Wherever I have to!" she said Frantically, "I will search every stone in this country if I have to."

"And you would find nothing," said Grendan. "Stop a moment and think about it. Have you ever slept in so late? It's almost noon. Also how do you think I realized they were gone? I was in a half trance when a voice spoke to me. We have to take a different path now. We are needed on other issues."

"But they are too young to be out on their own," said Elizabeth.

"They are not on their own," said Grendan. "It was a strong magic to set today's events in motion and they will have a guardian sent to them, but that must fall to somebody else now."

Elizabeth gave way. She knew Grendan was right. He was always right. They had no idea what direction Dolan had went or how much of a head start he had.

"I swear if anything happens to them......" she said giving him a look.

Grendan just shook his head in agreement. He had the job of letting the Wizard council know of the events, and he would much rather deal with them now than Elizabeth if something happened.

Grendan sat in a chair across the table from

Falcor, trying to read the wizards expressions, without any luck. Falcor was calm and deep in thought and Grendan wasn't sure if this was a good sign or not.

Finally, the old Wizard spoke. "They would have had to have help getting out of the city unnoticed. But if it's like you say and Kaylar was behind it, then it would have happened anyways. And with the news I received this morning we have bigger problems to deal with.

This caught Grendan off guard. "What news?" he asked.

"Jo-El and his army is preparing to move out and it looks like they are coming this way," said Falcor.

"Kryan must be really getting bold to move against Camaroon," said Grendan

"I'm not so sure he is truly in charge," answered Falcor. "It's looking like Jo-el is the one calling the shots and Kryan is just a puppet leader."

"Has this been confirmed or is it just speculation?" asked Grendan.

"I am waiting on confirmation," said Falcor,

"But I am calling the council together in the morning. I would like to do it sooner, but some have already left to go back to their dealings they have had going on. I can't get them back here before morning."

"In the meantime, are we going to start preparing for the worst?" asked Grendan.

"We are at least going to be putting people on alert," said Falcor, "But I don't want to sound an alarm just yet. I don't want panic."

"I must go let the others know what is going on?" said Grendan.

"Don't tell them too much," said Falcor, " I would rather you not tell them anything, but I know you well enough to know that wouldn't happen."

Grendan headed back to their apartment. He was thinking about how much time had been wasted here with meetings. He hated meetings because all that seemed to get accomplished was this one or that one wanted more information. They had already been here for weeks and how much information had already been overlooked. How long had the Army been preparing. He knew it was bad not to think things through and act too soon, but it was also bad to overthink something.

When he joined the others in the common room of their apartment, he explained what Falcor had told him. He also told them his concerns that there was more to this than could be seen on the surface. He couldn't help but think that Jo-el had more going on than they knew about.

"I should go and sound the alarm with my people," said Flanagan. "I know how wizards want to analyze everything and I myself would rather prepare for the worst and it not happen then have it come back to bite me in the keister."

"I agree with Flanagan," said Layana. "I will go to the council of my people. If the Quantuan army is already moving to mobilize then we will be behind."

"I feel we need more than the Elves, Dwarfs and guards of Camaroon to deal with this," said Grendan.

"Do you not think we can handle the likes of Jo-el?" said Flanagan.

"I fear there may be more to what's coming than what we see," said Grendan. "There is a deeper darker magic at work here. There are things that have been forgotten about and have become myth and lore that could be at work here."

Grendan didn't elaborate any further. He just sat back and set himself to thought. The others talked back and forth about what might be expected. It was starting to get late in the evening, and they were getting ready for the evening meal.

They were served a moderate meal though none really had an appetite. They ate in silence. Even Flanagan didn't eat any more than three servings and all of them skipped desert. After all the dishes were cleared away, they sat around the table still.

Finally, Grendan broke the silence. "I think Elizabeth and I should travel west."

"What is west?" asked Elizabeth.

"We may find help with the Plainsmen and the Riders from the mountains," said Grendan.

"Do you really think they would help?" asked Flanagan. "I mean the plainsmen it's possible, but the mountain people have always kept to themselves."

"They were once strong allies," said Grendan, "But because the rest of Amergon distrusted them, some even to the point of telling lies to make them look bad, they began to distrust and withdrew to their mountains."

"But wouldn't people see through the lies?" asked Elizabeth.

"It is easier to believe a lie than the truth," said Grendan

"Yes, and I know people that would rather climb a tree to lie than stand on the ground to tell the truth," said Flanagan.

"I think we should each go to one," said Grendan, "I don't think we have time for us both to go together to them."

"I agree," replied Elizabeth.

They started preparing to leave. They decided to wait until they were out in the city to get the traveling rations they would need so it didn't take long to be ready. Once they were, then they made their way to the front entrance and out into the city. Flanagan and Layana bid them farewell after they left the little shop and made their way to the east gate and headed home to warn the

Dwarves and the Elves. Grendan and Elizabeth went to the west gate.

"We can travel together until we reach the Dragons pass, " said Grendan, "then I shall turn southwest to the plains lands."

"Are you sure the mountain people will listen to me?" asked Elizabeth.

"I'm hoping so," said Grendan. "The plainsmen are not so apt to. They feel women should remain in the home and bare children, so it is unlikely that you would get much more past the front gate."

It was a day and a half to the Dragons Pass and was very un-eventful. There had been patches of rain that had left muddy areas in the road that Grendan seemed to barely notice. But Elizabeth was wearing a traveling gown that even though it was warm and didn't hinder her walking the long distance, it seemed to catch every drop of mud on the path. She knew this was an exaggeration, but it didn't make it any easier.

When they reached the pass, it was close to night fall the following day. They had decided to travel all night the night before but they both knew the next step of their journey required them to rest. Neither trail would be easy. Elizabeth's would be steep and rocky while Grendan's would be dry and hot. So, they settled in for the night. Neither one feeling much like talking.

When Flanagan left Layana a few miles outside the gate, he set himself to a sturdy pace towards home. He had been ready for battle but now he had time to think about it and he dreaded what was to come. Not because of the battling but because he knew he would lose good friends if not the good friends losing him. He chuckled a little at the thought that old Briganty would probably miss him the most since he spent most of his pay at his tavern either in drinks or repairs.

Layana made her way through the forest. She didn't want this upcoming war, but she knew there wasn't anything she could do about it. She detested war, the smell of death that was to come with it. She had been in some skirmishes and the smell of blood filled the air then. It would be far worse this time. How could anybody find glory in battle? It was a necessity at time but far from glorious.

CHAPTER 11
UNEXPECTED GARDIAN

It was late when Dolan and his companions reached the small village at the base of the mountain range. The streets were empty and quiet. They made their way to the Inn. They were all looking forward to getting to sleep in a bed for a change. Even though they were anxious to get some decent rest, they stood in the shadows outside listening to the conversation coming from the tavern that was below the rooms of the Inn.

"I'm telling you they are looking for a woman and a boy!" A man was saying half slurring his words as he spoke.

"Well I'm just looking for a woman, I have no interest in any boys," said another man with a deep mocking laugh.

"Maybe so," said the other man, "But I bet you would be interested in the gold they are offering for them."

"Well now," said the man as he stopped laughing. "That does change things a bit. "

"Thought that might get your attention Delmar," said the first man.

"Well I tell you Kor," Delmar said getting more serious, "If I can make money from a woman instead of her costing me money, I am all for it."

It was Kor's turn to laugh now. "Delmar that will defiantly be a change."

Delmar started to protest but then went silent for a few minutes. After a bit of thought he looked at Kor with pure soberness and asked, "What more can you tell me?"

"Well," Kor started explaining what he could remember through the fuzziness in his head. "They are traveling with a Wizard and a Dwarf. And they may have picked up an Elven woman along the way."

Dolan and his companions slipped out of earshot during this part of the conversation and made their way into the ally beside the Inn. When they figured they were back far enough not to be seen, they huddled close to the building to discuss what they should do.

"Okay this is not good," said Dolan.

"Not at all," Renee said

"Any suggestions?" asked Dolan.

"I think we should move on," said Yardell. "Renee could pass as an Elven woman to two drunks and except for having Edward and not Lady Elizabeth, they described our little group quite well."

"That is true now that you mention it," said Dolan.

"But it's cold and I'm hungry," said Edward.

"I know, and so are we," said Renee gently. "But we don't have any other choice."

"Maybe we can help you with that." Came a voice from the front of the ally.

Dolan recognized the voice as Delmar from the bar and his blood ran cold. They had apparently been able to hear them whispering when they had left the bar. Dolan looked about and his heart sank when he noticed that the only way out of this ally was through the two drunk men.

"We know a nice warm place where you can get all the rest you want," Delmar was saying. "And it won't cost you a dime."

"Well at least you won't have to pay them anything," added Kor with a chuckle.

They started advancing on the small company. Dolan noticed one of them had a large stick in his hand and he could barely make out the shape of a knife in the others hand. Dolan and Yardell took up positions in front of the others. He felt they had a chance to defend themselves. He soon lost that feeling when another form emerged from the shadows behind Delmar and Kor. They had brought a companion and there was no mistake of the shape of a sword in his hand.

Suddenly the unknown man swung his sword and the three stopped their advancement. There was no movement at all for what seemed to be ages, then Dolan noticed That Kor and Delmar were sinking to the ground, and then they collapsed without a sound. Dolan was speechless. In fact, nobody made a sound until a strong study voice cut the silence

"Renee, Edward, are you two okay?" said the voice.

"Uncle is that you?" asked Renee

"Yes." Came the reply

Renee and Edward ran up to the man and hugged him, and he wrapped his arms around them.

"Come we must leave here before we are seen," said the man.

Dolan did not ask any questions, although he wanted to. He just started following Renee, Edward and their new companion. He was a large man that seemed to favor his left side when he walked. Dolan could not get a good look at his face, but found something familiar about him. He could not place where he had seen him before.

They walked down the street a short distance and turned the corner. After they had traveled a little further, they made another turn. Soon Dolan had lost count of the turns and the directions that they had turned. They had been walking about thirty minutes or so when they came to a small cottage. The man led them to the front door and walked inside.

They stepped inside to much needed warmth. It had seemed to be getting colder by the hour the more they traveled north. Dolan scanned his surroundings to find nothing that seemed out of the ordinary or extremely dangerous. It was a quaint little front room with moderate furnishings. Nothing extreme or out of the ordinary.

"I am so happy to see you uncle!" Renee was saying when Dolan realized she was talking. "Dolan this is Uncle Loetaun."

Suddenly realization set in and Dolan knew where he had seen this man before. He wanted to run but stood frozen. Everyone except Loetaun was looking at him puzzled. None of the others had been there that night when he and his mother had to flee the valley for their lives. They did not know that it was Loetaun they had been running from. It was Loetaun that Dolan had thought was dead by Flanagan's hand. Yet here he stood in front of him, although it was apparent that he was not the same after their first meeting as he was at the beginning of it.

"We have met," said Loetaun in a forced calm voice.

"Yes, we have," agreed Dolan. "Are you planning on turning me over to your men?"

"Much has changed since our last meeting young one," said Loetaun. "For one, I no longer have my men. I am now hunted just like you."

"How can I believe that?" Dolan asked, "You tried so hard before and was so set to take me and my mother."

"What are you talking about Dolan?" asked Renee.

"This is the man that chased me and my mother from our home." answered Dolan.

A look of shock came over Renee. "You must be mistaken," she said.

"He's partly righ,." said Loetaun. "I was sent to retrieve them, but I was not among the ones that went to their home. That was a regiment of regular soldiers. I was a member of the scouts. I have heard what happened at your home and I would have handled it quite differently.The fact is that had been my scout division we would not be at this point we are at now."

"Was it your men?" asked Renee fighting back tears. "Was it your men that killed my parents?"

Loetaun had a look of anguish crossed with anger. "No. I do not know who was behind that. Were you there? I need you to tell me everything."

They all found seats and Renee started telling of the events that had happened to Edward and herself. It was hours before they finished telling him most of everything up to this point. Dolan and Yardell both made it a point to omit certain information, especially if it pertained to Cameroon. Dolan did not trust Loetaun. For all he knew Loetaun was there to gather information.

"Can you tell me anything else about the men that attacked you at the farmhouse?" Loetaun asked.

"I told you everything I can think of," said Renee. She was sitting on the fireplace hearth. Edward was asleep with his head laying in her lap.

"What about their clothes?" pressed Loetaun.

"It was dark so I couldn't tell you anything except they had on Leather," answered Renee.

"I did notice something," said Dolan. "There was a serpent wrapped around a ball stamped in the leather."

"Are you sure?" asked Loetaun.

"Yes," answered Dolan. "I hate snakes so that image stuck out, but I didn't think anything of it. Does it mean anything?"

"It's a symbol of their order," said Loetaun. "The ball represents the moon. The serpent represents the armies of Jo-El. He figures on ruling over all the lands that the moon covers. They are the most elite and ruthless of all his troops. I just knew I was supposed to retrieve you and take you to my superiors, and that is all I was told. If he has his elite troops looking for you also then you must be of major importance. What are you not telling me?"

"I have told you all that I can," answered Dolan

"I don't like having things held back!" Loetaun said sternly.

"I don't like being hunted!" said Dolan trying to be stern.

"Neither do I," Loetaun said.

"Well here we are then," said Dolan. "Both hunted and neither trusting to tell everything."

Dolan did not know why he said what he did. He was not even sure Loetaun was holding anything back, but he felt it was the right thing to say. Loetaun sat looking Dolan up and down. Dolan held firm even though he felt like running.

"I think we all should get some rest," said Renee, breaking the tension.

"Very well," said Loetaun after a moment. "I will show you to your sleeping cots."

Loetaun stood to show them to where they could sleep. Dolan got a good look at the man for the first time. He was a large man with broad shoulders. His stern chiseled face was fierce looking probably more so with the battle scars on his left side.

Dolan went to bed and soon fell asleep. He hadn't been asleep long before he felt himself moving through the streets of the village. He soon found himself standing at the mouth of the alley where they had met up with Loetaun earlier that night. There was still blood puddled on the bricks.

Dolan walked back towards the back of the alley where he saw a form standing. As he drew closer he recognized the man standing there. It was Kaylar

"Hello Dolan." said Kaylar.

"I'm surprised to see you here." said Dolan.

"I needed to let you know a little more." Kaylar said

"I have been wondering if I was heading the right direction." said Dolan.

"You have come to the exact place you needed to." Kaylar told him. "Now the rest of the way will be a little more difficult."

"The difficult thing is going to be getting away from Loetaun." said Dolan.

"You need to bring him with you." Said Kaylar.

"But he's the one that was hunting us." said Dolan

"Yes but now he's going to be your protector." said Kaylar.

"Why would I protect him?" said a voice from behind Dolan

Dolan turned to see Loetaun standing at the mouth of the alley. He had a puzzled look on his face. Dolan figured he was trying to figure out if he was dreaming or not.

"Welcome Loetaun." said Kaylar. "Do you think you are here by choice?"

"I came here looking for Renee and Edward." said Loetaun. "Now that I have found them we are going to go someplace safe."

"You know that there is no place that is safe." said Kaylar. "You are being hunted and Renee has already set her mind to complete her journey. If you want to keep them safe you will go with them."

Loetaun's expression went cold as he stared at Kaylar. After a few tense moments he gave way.

"I will go and keep Renee and Edward safe." Loetaun said coldly. "I will protect Dolan as long as it doesn't hinder that."

"You both must go back soon." said Kaylar. "Tomorrow you will need to head up the mountain and make for Stone Haven."

With that Dolan found himself back at the cottage waking up in bed. He got up and went to the fireplace and stirred the coals. Moments latter he realized that Loetaun was standing behind him.

"That wasn't just a dream was it?" Loetaun said as Dolan turned to face him.

"No it wasn't." said Dolan

"I meant what I said." said Loetaun. "I will protect you as long as Renee and Edward are not put in danger."

"I wouldn't want it any other way." said Dolan

With that they both went back to bed. They knew it wasn't going to be easy to reach where they were going.

CHAPTER 12
WAR COUNCIL

Jo-Ele sat half listening to his generals. He wished he didn't have to go through all this just to have what he wanted done carried out in the end anyways. But he did find out things during these little sessions. Granted usually it was that he had superior intellect. But every now and then there was something he could use.

"We have started troops moving toward Cameroon" one of the Generals was saying

"I still don't understand why we are only moving a quarter of the troops." Another one said

"I don't see why I am expected to explain." Jo-Ele said calmly "General Krorg do you care to explain since you are usually the one that pays the most attention to me."

Krorg sat next to Jo-Ele. He was a large man who had seen his share of battle. He leaned forward cupping his hands together as he started speaking. "We only want them thinking we are moving to attempt to take the city. We have the rest of our troops scattered out but not too thin. That way the size of our army is not fully known. We won't be moving fully until our allies join us."

They discussed more tactics and strategies for the next several hours until Jo-El grew tired of all the chatter and brought the meeting to an end. After everybody had gone he stood at a huge table and looked over the maps laid out on it. He had studied these maps so much that he could read them in the dark. But he still studied them as if something was going to change and more would be revealed to him.

He was lost in his thought when he heard something behind him, when he turned He saw the tall form of a man standing in the corner. He knew it was Kieser without anything being said. He never knew when Kieser would show up but it was always when his talents were required.

"I was disappointed that my wishes wasn't carried out." Jo-Ele said.

"I owed it to him." said Kieser

"How can I trust that you will carry out what needs to be done now?" Asked Jo-Ele

"I only owed it to him one time." Answered Kieser.

"I hope so, I would hate to have to add another name to the list." Said Jo-Ele.

"That would be a name that would never be stricken from that list." Kieser said coldly

"I can find somebody better than you." said Jo-Ele.

"If you will remember you tried that one time before." said Kieser. "And you must have forgotten are conversation after that."

"I haven't forgotten anything!" Jo-Ele said feeling the anger rising in him. "I also don't take threats well."

"I don't usually give warnings." said Kieser. "I won't do it again."

"I think we should get back on subject." said Jo-Ele. "I want the situation taken care of quickly. I don't want him just dead. Bring him back so he can be executed in public. I want anybody who thinks they can get away with this to know otherwise."

Jo-Ele turned and walked back to the table with the maps. "Is that clear?" He said turning to look at Kieser again. But he was speaking to empty darkness. The man was gone as quick as he had appeared. He hated that but it was to be expected with an assassin. And Kieser was the best there was he couldn't dismiss that. He was the only one Jo-Ele knew that could have slipped in here without his personal guard knowing anything about it.

As Kieser slipped through the shadows of the camp past soldiers who had no idea he was even alive he pondered how easy it would be to end this war before it even began. He could eliminate the entire command structure including the emperor in one night and never be caught. But that wasn't for him to do. Somebody else would just rise to power and he would have to do it all over again, besides these fools paid him handsomely for his work.

He had a stop to make before carrying out his assignment. Kryen wasn't expecting him but he would be interested in what he had to say. Besides he enjoyed dropping by unexpectedly that's how he was able to find out stuff.

Kryen was sleeping soundly lost in his dreams. He knew he was dreaming even though he was asleep. For some reason he always knew it was a dream. Sometimes he could control the dream even. But he could never remember his dreams after he woke. They would flee his mind like the wind blowing through his chamber window.

It was the this later that woke him. The chill of the morning air cutting into him and making him uncomfortable. He didn't like being uncomfortable and he would make sure that the servant that had opened the window would be even more uncomfortable.

He reached for the cord to ring the bell for his servant and couldn't find it. Reluctantly he lifted the covers from over his head to look for the elusive cord that was supposed to be right next to his bed. He had never had problems finding it before. But for some reason it was not there.

"It's not there." said a voice. "We don't need to be disturbed."

Kryen knew the voice instantly. Even though he rarely heard it. Yet he always looked forward to these talks. He learned so much when Keiser would visit him. His subjects thought he was some kind of fool and he was glad to let them think that right now. The time would come to show them who was in charge but not yet.

"What news do you bring me?" Kryen asked

"Your armies are preparing for war." Answered Kieser

"That's old news." said Kyren. "I need to know what's current."

"Jo-Ele is seeking help from the Dark Elves of the Marsh lands." said Kieser. "He has also recruited the Orcs and has part of the Giants on his side."

"I knew that I wasn't getting full reports." said Kyren. "I feel he is more ambitious than I thought. He will be setting his eyes on my throne before long. I need you to be prepared if he does."

"I already figured I would be taking care of the situation." said Kieser. "I have warned you of this before and would have already taken care of it if allowed."

"I know my friend." said Kyren. "But I still need him to fulfill the next step. He has a way of controlling the armies that I have never seen before. He is the best at warfare."

"As you wish." said Kieser "Watch yourself though. I have had to remove a couple obstacles that has come up against you."

"I did not know this." said Kyren

"You didn't need to at the time." said Kieser. "But you do need to understand that even though they are not as efficient as I am there is other assassins than me. And they don't have the same plans and ideas that I do."

"I take it you were compensated for your work?" said Kyren

"Yes." Answered Kieser. "And on that note if you execute the treasurer every time the books are off then your going to run out of qualified people."

"I will remember that." said Kyren. "But I have to make some kind of example."

"Well may a suggest that you just do a public flogging tomorrow to your current one." said Kieser.

Kyren gave him a look and shook his head. He wanted to ask for details but decided to let it go. He knew he really didn't want to know anything else. He had gotten a couple glasses out and poured them both drinks. They sat in silence for a while enjoying the warmth of the liquor they were drinking.

"I will be out of reach for a while." said Kieser after a few minutes.

"Do I need to be worried?" Kyren asked.

"No." Said Kieser. "I have made arrangements for your protection. But it will be my fee plus a little more."

"I can deal with that." said Kyren.

"You should get rest now." said Kieser. "I must go and take care of things."

Kyren just nodded and walked back to his bed. He turned to say something but found he was alone in his room. It un-nerved him when Kieser would come and go like that but he knew it was part of him. He would never give up what made him so effective in his job.

This time when Kieser was leaving he felt a sadness in him. He kind of liked Kyren and hoped he got the order from him first. He knew that Jo-Ele would give him the order to kill Kyren. The question was who would place the order first.

Now he had to go and hunt an old friend down. That was one of the draw backs about his profession, if a job along he had to take it no matter who it was.   He could refuse but that would effect future assignments. So no matter how much he didn't want to he would follow through with what he had been contracted to do.

www.ingramcontent.com/pod-product-compliance
Lightning Source LLC
Chambersburg PA
CBHW072225150726
48002CB00005B/1949